The Summer of '61
By Heather Roberson

ISNB9798647127990

To all who remember their first love.

1

PRESENT DAY

Grandma slipped off her rubber boots in the breezeway then set the basket full of eggs on the kitchen counter. The cool touch of the linoleum floor on her bare feet sent a little chill over her aging body. The smell of coffee and warm cornbread filled the kitchen as she inspected each egg while listening to the chipper clucks from the hens outside. Gazing out the window above the sink, she watched them as they pecked the ground for bugs and grain. Big Red, the handsome rooster of the barnyard, would soon be making his morning announcement.

Grandma took the cast iron pans from the bottom drawer of the stove. Running her fingers on the inside, she made sure they were nice and greasy. One was used for scrambling the eggs. In the other, she laid strips of bacon she had gotten from the neighboring farm down the road. It was their last pig, Wilber. Over the last few years, the small town was growing into a city. Companies were buying up properties and building apartments, condominiums, and strip malls on the land that generations before had laboriously plowed.

Grandma and Grandpa purchased the house about twenty years ago. According to public records, this fourth of July would mark the house's one hundred and thirteenth birthday. Sadly, today, nothing was left of the barns or silos except for rocky foundations and partial walls. A rusted old tractor that used to plow the cornfields, was now a permanent decoration in the corner of the yard with vines hiding some of it. Grandpa swore he would never give up his land to those corporate assholes. The only things that resembled the farm now were the dozen or so chickens and a few ducks named after the seven dwarfs that wandered the yard freely.

As Grandma took the cornbread out of the oven, she heard the screen door on the front porch slam shut as stomping feet ran through the dining room and into the kitchen.

"Hi Grandma," the sisters said in unison. "Is breakfast ready yet?" Hayleigh asked. She was a spunky and driven girl. She had been at the top of her class since the sixth grade and fully intended to keep this rank through this, sophomore year of high school. She loved science and had dreams of going to the best medical school in the state, the University of Wisconsin in Madison.

"Good morning, girls. Breakfast is just about ready. Heidi, be a dear and throw bread in the toaster will you?"

"Sure thing Grandma," Heidi replied as she took the bread out of the bread box. Heidi was the shy type. She was born to be a musician and was excellent at drawing. It was the summer before her freshman year in high school. She was babysitting for a few families in town and saving up money. It was her dream to someday visit some of the finest art museums in Paris.

"Where are your mother and father, Hayleigh?"

"Aunt Tammy and Uncle Alex and the twins followed us up the driveway. So I'm sure they are all outside chatting and unloading the car."

"Hi, Grandma, where do you want these ears of corn?" Nicholas asked as he entered the kitchen with an armful of bags stuffed with ears of corn.

"Grandma, where do you want me to put all these beans?" Nathan asked as he bounced in behind his brother. Nicholas and Nathan were identical twins. Nicholas was the captain of the high school swim team while Nathan was a star athlete on the track team. He broke several records in the 400-meter race and the hurdles. Although both were only juniors in high school, colleges were already scouting both of them. There was no doubt both boys were getting a free ride to college.

"You boys can put all those on the picnic table outside," their mom Tammy answered, as she and her round pregnant belly waddled into the kitchen.

"Grandma, why do we have to be here so early?" Hayleigh yawned, "Big Red is just now cock-a-doodle-dooing. It's summer vacation. I should be sleeping in."

"Because the early bird catches the worm. Or in this case, the early fish catches the worm." Grandpa said as he and his cane slowly descended the last of the steps from upstairs.

"Morning Grandpa." Heidi and Hayleigh said together.

"Morning my darlings. Did you all bring your fishing poles?"

"We sure did Grandpa," Nathan said as he and Nicholas came backside, followed by their dad Alex and Hayleigh and Heidi's parents, Delilah and Stanley.

"Great. Now let's eat so we can get going," Grandpa said limping to the spread of breakfast food on the dining room table, "This smells delicious buttercup," he told Grandma as he kissed her on the cheek before he sat at the head of the table.

When all the family was finally seated at the dining room table Grandpa had made several years back, they all held hands and he gave thanks to the Lord for his wonderful family. When his first grandchild was born,

Grandpa knew the family was going to continue to grow, so he went into the woods at the edge of the property and chopped down the biggest oak tree he could find. It took him a year to make the tree into the table the family was sitting at today.

As soon as their bellies were full, Grandpa would be taking his grandkids down the path to the stream just beyond the place where that big oak tree once stood. He and his grandkids were going to fish for their lunch, while Grandma and her two daughters, Tammy and Delilah, would wash the breakfast dishes and begin to prepare for their Fourth of July dinner. Their husbands, Alex and Stanley, would clean up the yard, move picnic tables, and set up the yard games.

The sun was beating down on the earth by ten o'clock in the morning when all the kids came running up the path with their abundant catch of the day, their grandpa quickly limping behind.

Stanley had just positioned a huge cast iron pot on the chains over the fire pit. The corn had just been husked and set aside until the water in the pot was boiling.

Alex started filleting the great stream catch of the day, while Stanley began hanging a grate from chains over a second fire pit. Tammy cut the watermelon and muskmelon she and her sister Delilah had picked from the garden five minutes before. Grandma made pie crust and peeled the apples for the apple pie while Delilah cut green beans and threw them in a pot then prepared the potato salad.

After the grandchildren had washed their hands, they covered the picnic tables with red and white checkered vinyl tablecloths. They then chased the chickens and ducks around the yard like they did when they were younger.

By noon, everyone was gathered around the picnic tables, quickly devouring the meal that took a few hours to prepare. As their bellies expanded, dark ominous clouds gathered in the sky. Thunder rumbled in the distance.

"Maybe we should start getting everything inside," Grandma announced.

"It's just a mid-afternoon storm." her husband said, loosening his belt, "No need to rush. It's still to the west of us."

"Grandma is right." Delilah chimed in, "Come on kids, everybody grab something from the table and head inside."

All the girls screamed as a bolt of lightning hit the earth about three miles from the farm. As a crack of thunder rolled across the sky, Grandma helped pregnant Tammy waddle to the house, while Hayleigh, Heidi, and their mom ran to the house with their arms full of dishes of food.

"Aw come on, it's just a thunderstorm," The twins scoffed.

"Your Grandma is right boys," Alex said, "Grab something and get inside."

As everyone made their way inside, Grandma turned on the television. The local channel had been interrupted from their regularly scheduled program to the local news for a weather alert. The screen was lit up with oranges, yellows, and deep reds.

"A line of severe storms is heading east. These storms are producing strong winds and golf ball size hail. It's best to stay indoors and away from windows." The forecaster announced.

"Do you think we can still shoot off fireworks tonight Grandpa?" Nicholas asked.

"I am certain of it, child. These storms will blow through pretty quick."

Suddenly the loud weather warning beep came across the television.

"This just in," the forecaster said frantically, "A tornado has been spotted on the ground. If you are in the towns of Maple Grove, Juddville, Fish Creek, Gibraltar, and Ephraim take cover immediately. I repeat a tornado is on the ground. Take cover immediately."

"Oh no, that's us," Tammy exclaimed. "Quick everyone down in the cellar."

2

The only way into the cellar was through ground doors outside of the farmhouse. Grandpa and Stanley lifted the heavy doors against the wind, while Alex and one of his sons helped everyone down the narrow cement steps.

"What about the chickens and ducks?" screamed Hayleigh as her hair whipped around her face.

"They'll be fine," her cousin Nicholas yelled.

Once everybody was in the cellar, Grandpa and Stanley tried to close the doors up above. But the wind was too strong. Everyone screamed as one of the doors went flying into the storm.

"Quick, into that corner. Everybody squeeze in as tight as you can," Delilah yelled, The Grandpa and the other men used themselves as human shields to protect the women and four kids. Rain poured in from where the door once was. The wind roared like a freight train as the tornado passed by.

Suddenly there was a loud crash from outside.

"Oh my Gosh. What was that?" Grandma yelled. The rafters on the ceiling began to shake with tremendous force. One of the iron pipes broke, shooting water everywhere. Stanley and Alex took off their shirts and tried to plug the pipes while Grandpa searched frantically in the dim light for the shutoff valve. Nicholas and Nathan tried to shield their pregnant mother from the spraying water.

And then just like that, Grandpa turned the water off and all was calm outside. In the cellar, no one moved or said a peep as fear still clung to everyone huddled in the corner.

"Hey, be cautious," Stanley suggested as he and Alex followed their father-in-law up and out of the cellar. "We don't know what kind of damage there may be."

Thunder still rumbled in the distance as everyone carefully made their way out of the cellar and surveyed the damage. The sun shone in a bright blue sky. A cool breeze blew and the birds chirped away as though nothing had happened. The cast-iron pots still stood over the fire pits unscathed by the storm. The picnic tables, where everyone had been eating lunch not twenty minutes ago, were tipped on their sides. The red and white checkered tablecloths were caught on the rocks of the firepits, flapping gently in the breeze.

"Oh, Grandpa, our house," Grandma shrieked, with her hands on her chest, almost in tears.

Everyone looked in her direction. A big gaping hole now appeared in the house where the living room was. Sitting before them, almost untouched by the storm, was the antique rocking chair that had tipped over and pictures hanging on the wall were now a little cockeyed. Patches, the family cat, was on the couch. His back arched, his tail all puffed out, and his claws holding tight to the cushion as he hissed at the displaced chicken, Gertrude. The white lace curtains on the windows danced back and forth as they normally would on a breezy summer afternoon.

"Well buttercup, you always said you wanted a sliding glass door and a wrap-around porch added on. Now I have a little less work to do," Grandpa joked, trying to lighten the sorrowful mood.

"And I guess we are all getting new vehicles?" Nathan asked, unsure of his thoughts.

Everyone looked towards the driveway. The 150-year-old oak tree that had withstood all other storms, now lay uprooted upon the cars parked in the driveway. And the partially rusted red tractor that was entangled in weeds in the corner of the yard now had a new home in the branches.

"That loud crashing noise must have been when the tractor hit the house," Hayleigh said.

"And the tree falling," Heidi added, getting her cell phone out of her pocket.

"Well, I guess we should start by taking pictures and calling our insurance companies," Tammy suggested, but everyone already had their cell phones out, snapping pictures of the damage.

"I guess we have extra wood for our bonfire tonight, right Grandpa?" Hayleigh asked.

"We will see." He sighed, looking at the path of trees that were down, from the house to the stream. "Boys, why don't you carefully get the chainsaws out of the garage and make sure we have enough gas in them. Alex, go with them please and see if you can find a blue tarp or two so we can cover up that hole on the side of the house."

"What about us?" Heidi and Hayleigh asked.

"Girls, go in the shed and hook up the small trailers to the four-wheelers. We are going to need them. But EVERYONE be careful. There could be more damage," Grandpa warned.

Once Grandpa delegated everything, the men and grandkids started clearing debris from the yard. Grandma cautiously made her way through the open hold in the living room and shooed the chicken out of the house and calmed down the cat. Then she went into the kitchen and made lemonade for everyone. She did everything in her willpower to keep from crying as she heard disappointing sighs come from her daughters as they sat on the porch and talked to their insurance agents.

Grandma stared out the kitchen window and counted her blessings, so much damage but not a scratch on any of her loved ones. This for sure will be a Fourth of July to remember, she thought to herself. The telephone poles were leaning and barely hanging on to their lines for as far as the eye could see. She prayed to the Lord that her neighbors were okay.

"There are more storms coming. Where is everyone?" Delilah yelled in panic as thunder rumbled in the distance.

"I just saw them take a load of debris down towards the woods," Grandma answered, walking out onto the porch.

"These storms are weakening Delilah, " Tammy remarked looking at the weather update on her cell phone, "It won't be as bad as last time."

"I wonder if Alex ever found the tarp?" Grandma said quietly, "We need to get this hole covered before any more rain gets in and ruins the living room completely."

"I guess we should go look for Alex. The sooner this hole is covered, the better," Tammy said, "I wonder if the tents are still in the shed too? I don't think we will be able to sleep in the house tonight."

As the women made their way off the porch, more thunder rumbled in the distance. Dark clouds were beginning to gather once again.

"We best walk fast," Grandma suggested.

"Nicholas...Nathan!" Tammy yelled for her sons. But it was no use. The wind muffled her cries.

"Look, over there! By the barn!" Tammy announced as she pulled Delilah's arm and guided the ladies in her direction.

As Grandma and her daughters came nearer to the barn, they noticed everyone was huddled over Hayleigh and a hollow tree trunk.

"What on earth are you all doing?" Delilah said in a panic. "There are more storms heading our way. We have to get that hole in the house covered quickly."

"Look, Mom! Look what Hayleigh found in the tree trunk," Heidi urged for her mom to come closer.

"We don't have time to be gawking at a book," Delilah cried. "Get your butts back to the house now, before we get caught out in these storms."

"Calm down, Honey," Stanley said, grabbing his wife's hand. "Hayleigh, why don't you bring the book back to the house and we will all have a look at it."

"Your father is right, Hayleigh," her uncle Alex said, "we need to hurry. Those clouds are getting darker and the wind is picking up."

Tammy and Grandpa rode on the back of the four-wheeler while everyone else quickly ran back to the house.

Once back at the house, Stanley and Alex covered the big hole with the tarps. Grandpa searched the shed for the tents that would be their sleeping quarters for just tonight. Grandma poured lemonade for the rest of the family as they sat on the porch admiring Hayleigh's treasure.

"I bet it's over one hundred years old!" Nicholas said excitedly.

"Oh, I bet it belongs to that Iverson guy we learned about in history class," Nathan replied.

"You both are wrong," Hayleigh said as she peered at the first page. "it's only from 1961. Man, that's so lame. I thought we had actually found something cool."

"Oh cool, it's a hippy's book. Maybe it has the secret to finding inner happiness."

"Shut up Nicholas. You're so dumb," Hayleigh replied, rolling her eyes at her cousin.

"Now hold on," Tammy said as she took the book from Hayleigh. "This is something special," she said, flipping the pages carefully. "It's someone's diary. And the fact that the owner went through a lot of trouble to hide it in the tree trunk means something."

"Ooh! Juicy secrets," Heidi said as she sat her lemonade down. "Read it, Aunt Tammy, read it!"

3

Thursday, May 25, 1961

Dear Diary,

I am so mad. Georgie and I had made plans to go to the picnic at the pond and then walk up to the outlook with all of our friends. But tonight he told me he had to work at the ice cream shop because everyone else has asked off. Why can't his boss, Mr. Davis, tell his employees they can't take off the first weekend of summer? Why does my boyfriend always have to be the suck up? Now I will be the only one at the picnic without a date.

Wilma shut her pink floral diary and put the key lock through the link and pushed up until she heard a click. She tucked the diary under her mattress for safekeeping then tucked herself under blankets and turned out the lamp on her nightstand. She couldn't decide whether she was angry that Georgie had canceled a date on her again, or if she was happy and proud that Georgie was a mature responsible boy with a great work ethic that impressed her father. With a sigh, Wilma rolled over and reached for the teddy bear Georgie had won at the school carnival. The cologne he had sprayed on it still lingered as she sniffed the bear's head. With a smile on her lips, Wilma decided she couldn't be angry at Georgie for wanting to do the right thing. She hugged the teddy bear tightly and fell asleep.

The summer heat had made itself known the following afternoon as Wilma and her best friend, Maryanne, slowly walked home from school.

"Just because Georgie can't come to the picnic, you want to stay home?" Maryanne asked in disgust, "That's so lame Wilma. I mean, this is the start of summer. The first summer you and your dad aren't going on your California trip. The summer before our senior year of high school. And you just want to sit at home and wait on a guy?"

"Well, no. But what else am I supposed to do?" Wilma replied, "I mean you and Susan have dates. You all are going to be having fun and be all lovey-dovey at the picnic. And then what? You want me to tag along up to the lookout while you and Susan make out with your dates on the rocks? I don't think so."

The two friends walked in silence for a moment as others around them basked in the excitement of the last day of school. Dinging from bicycle bells sounded as kids on bikes hurried away from the school building. Whooshing and squeaking from the breaks of school buses filled the town as they stopped to let kids off.

"You know, I overheard Susan telling Sarah that Tommy told her he has his eye on you. What if I ask him to be your date for the picnic?"

Wilma rolled her eyes, "No thank you. I have a boyfriend. I'm not going to get fresh with another guy just because Georgie broke our date."

"Oh lighten up Wilma," Maryanne snorted as she ducked into an alleyway. She pulled a pack of cigarettes from her purse and lit one, inhaling deeply. "You and Georgie act like an old married couple. When are you ever going to let loose and have fun?" She asked, exhaling.

"We do not act like an old married couple," Wilma said as she waved her hand in the air trying to rid the smoke from Maryanne's cigarette. "Besides, a lot of couples get married and start their lives after graduation. So what."

"So what? Come on Wilma." Maryanne laughed, " It's a new decade. It's the 1960's. Not the 40's and 50's. The times are changing Wilma. We don't have to act like our parents."

Wilma sighed, "I have to get home. If I decide to go to the picnic tomorrow I will call you. But don't you dare ask Tommy to go with me," she said, waving a finger in Maryanne's face. She gave her friend that *don't you dare or else* look and walked away.

As she walked home she thought long and hard about what Maryanne said about her and Georgie acting like an old married couple. Would Georgie put a ring on her finger next year? Would Georgie move onto her grandpa's farm and take it over so it would stay in the family? Or would they move to a big city and become part of the hustle and bustle of modern life? She smiled at the thought of having at least five children with Georgie. She was an only child and at times that could get pretty lonely.

She was lost in thought as she turned onto the gravel road that led to her grandpa's farm. She and her father, William, had lived on the farm since she was a baby. For as long as she could remember, at the start of every summer, her father would pack the truck and they would head out west to California. William would show her the Naval base he used to be stationed at and would get one of the sailors to give them a tour of the massive ships. He would tell Wilma about his time in the Pacific during World War Two. Then they would walk around a quaint little neighborhood and visit the public library. And a few blocks after that, they would stop in front of a cute Tudor house built in the late 1920s. A tall white alder tree towered over the house in the backyard, while a small palm tree stood in the middle of the front yard and a flower bed with bright flowers lined the old house.

When Wilma was seven years old, she couldn't help but wonder why they visited the same places in California every summer. Her daddy was what people called country folk. She wondered why he was interested in the fancy library building and the funny looking house. So she asked him. She would never forget the look on her daddy's face as tears rolled down his cheeks when he told her the story of Gwendolyn, the woman he fell head over heels for in just a matter of three days.

Every summer from then on, Wilma and her father would stand in front of that Tudor house and Wilma would listen to the love story between her father and Gwendolyn. And then they would get back into the truck and drive three hours north to the Pine Woods Orphanage. Wilma learned at a young age that Gwendolyn, her birth mom, was forced to give her up for adoption. Gwendolyn had written William a letter telling him her father forced her to put their baby up for adoption. That was the last he had ever heard from her. He was discharged from the Navy three months later due to injuries he received when a kamikaze airplane crashed into his ship. When he returned to the states, he went to every orphanage in California, looking for the baby the letter described. He finally found Wilma and signed the papers that day, releasing her from the orphanage. He brought her home to live on his family farm and raised her with the help of his mom and dad. Every summer since then, William would take his daughter to California in hopes of maybe finding Gwendolyn.

This summer would be different. No more trips to California to stare at a house or public library. Last October, William had married Angela. Angela begged William to stop dwelling on the hopes of finding Gwendolyn. William's mother and father agreed as well. Grandpa needed help training all the boys coming from the surrounding towns for summer work on the farm.

Wilma was about to walk across the little bridge above a stream when she heard the dinging of a bicycle bell. She turned and saw Georgie racing up the gravel road. Her heart filled with joy as she waited for him.

"Hi, Babe," He huffed and puffed as he slowed his bike to a stop, "I saw these daisies on the side of the road and thought of you. I hope you're not mad about this weekend."

Wilma accepted the daisies, "It's fine. I think I'm just going to stay home. I don't want to feel like a third wheel since Susan and Maryanne both have dates."

"You are so wonderful Wilma," Georgie gleamed. "Can I call you after my shift tomorrow night? It will be around eight forty-five."

"You know my dad doesn't like phone calls after nine so you better call on time this time Georgie." Wilma smiled as she smelled the daisies.

Georgie positioned his bike so he could head home. He gave Wilma a quick peck on the cheek then smiled as he peddled away.

Wilma watched as Georgie darted out of the way of a line of four pickup trucks. Grandpa's summer help was arriving, honking and whipping up a cloud of dust as they made their way up the gravel road to the farm. As the last pickup truck passed her, a boy stuck his head out the window and smiled at her. As Wilma made her way back onto the road and up towards the farm, she noticed the boy kept his head out the window looking in her direction. Wilma smiled just for a second before laughing at herself. Other than Georgie, boys rarely found her attractive. Not a boy working on her grandpa's farm and certainly not Tommy. Geesh, Maryanne is such a great liar she thought out loud.

4

Sunday, May 28th, 1961

Dear Diary,

Everything works out for a reason. I am so glad I didn't go to the picnic. Susan told me the police came because there was a big fight. Apparently, it was over Maryanne. Ha, why am I not surprised? Susan said Maryanne was crying because she was so upset over the fight. But I bet my life savings, she was overjoyed that boys were fighting over her. Then Susan said after everything was said and done, Maryanne left in some random guy's car.

In happier news, Georgie is borrowing his parent's car tomorrow and driving down to Two Rivers. His parents own a small cottage there right on the lake. He asked me to go with him. Oh, how fun. Just me and my Georgie. I can't wait to wear my new polka dot bikini and the new halter dress I bought last week. I can't forget to pack the new cherry lip gloss I bought too. I need to wait for the perfect time to ask Father if I can go. I think I will do it right as we finish dinner tonight.

William wiped the corners of his mouth with the cloth napkin and loosened his belt just a bit.

"Mother, I don't know how you always do it, but the dinner tonight was wonderful. Don't you think so Angela?"

"Oh, indeed. Now that I am part of the family, Mrs. Barret, I would love to have your recipe."

"Angela, darling, how many times have I told you, please call me Mother. I am your mother-in-law now."

Angela looked down at her lap as she smiled a bit shy and embarrassed. William patted his wife's lap, "Give her time Mother. She will get to that point. In the meantime, let us get these dishes done up, shall we?"

"Oh, Grandma, that was a wonderful supper. Thank you," Wilma said, quickly standing up from her chair, "Angela, would you like to help me with the dishes?"

"Why of course dear. I would love to," Angela agreed as she wiped her mouth and put the cloth napkin on the table.

"Well, that is a change in events," Grandpa chuckled, "I wonder what she wants."

"Oh Father, why does she have to want something? She is growing into a responsible young adult. I'd like to believe we all did a great job of raising her."

"Ha! You may be a good father William, but you know nothing about raising kids, especially teenage girls," Grandma joked, "This is the first summer you haven't dragged her to California. This is the summer before her senior year in high school. Of course, she wants something."

Wilma sighed as she stared out the kitchen window, handing Angela a soapy plate, "Angela, did you ever go away with a boy when you were my age? Like, spend the night somewhere?"

Angela rinsed the soapy dish and dried it before answering, "Well, I turned eighteen during the summer of my senior year. So in a way, yes. His name was Johnny Clemons. Oh, he was so dreamy and…"

"Angela, can we get back to me, please? Georgie is getting his folks' car tomorrow and is going to Two Rivers to his family's cottage. He asked me to go."

"Well, you and Georgie have been together for a while. I don't see why not. Your father thinks he's a good boy. And his mother can't get enough of you. You are all she talks about when we have our ladies meeting down in the church basement."

"Oh God I know," Wilma scoffed, "Every time I go to Georgie's house, his mom talks about our wedding. He hasn't even proposed yet. Sometimes I just want to give her a knuckle sandwich."

Angela laughed as she dried another dish, "Oh come on Wilma, Mrs. Brown isn't that bad."

"No, I know. She's just annoying at times," Wilma paused, then asked, "Do you think Father will let me go to Two Rivers with Georgie?"

Wilma's step-mother sighed, "I think it sounds wonderful but you need to have a mature conversation with your father about it. How about you finish up here, and I'll try to butter him up for you?"

Leaving Wilma to finish washing the dishes, Angela walked quietly into the dining room. When her husband looked at her, she smiled. She undid the clasp of her hair clip and let her brunette hair fall past her shoulders. She ran her fingers through it, tossing strands of her hair left and right. She glanced at William and saw him staring at her with passion in his eyes. She knew what her husband liked. She then sauntered over to him and sat in his lap. Embarrassed that his parents saw this flirtatious side of his wife, he tried standing up but with no avail.

"Oh pardon us," His mother said, "it looks like you two want to be alone for a minute. Come on Henry, let's leave these two love birds alone."

After William's parents exited the dining room, Angela started to gently kiss William's neck and ear, "Honey, do you know what the best part about having children is?"

"Oh, and what would that be my dear?"

"Making them. Why don't we go up to the bedroom and start making one? I can put on that little outfit you like."

William chuckled a little bit. "I'm just about forty years old. Do you think I can raise another child?"

Angela rubbed her finger around his earlobe knowing that the sensation drove her husband wild. Then slowly unbuttoning his shirt, she replied, "Wilma will be married and starting her family in the next couple of years. Your father won't always be able to afford to pay those college boys to help run the farm. We need to produce more strong Barret babies to keep the farm going."

William began to relax as his wife's lips pressed up against his while her soft hands massaged his chest, "I don't know about more babies, but let's have some fun trying," He said as he gently pushed Angela off his lap and stood up. He wrapped his arms around her waist and kissed the back of her neck as he guided her in the direction of the stairs.

As they passed the kitchen, Wilma called out, "Hey Father, can I talk to you?"

"Not now Wilma. Can it wait until morning? Angela and I..."

"No. It's important. Please, Father?"

"Oh alright." William sighed. Holding his wife's hand, he kissed her on the lips, "Wait for me upstairs will you."

Angela bit her lip smiling and nodding her head, "Oh, and put that little outfit on for me." William whispered in her ear and slapped her on the ass as she headed up the stairs.

He watched as his wife walked up the stairs then headed into the kitchen, "What is so important that it can't wait until morning?"

"Well, Father. Um, well see um..." Wilma stammered nervously, "Well Georgie is going to Two Rivers tomorrow to his family cottage on Lake Michigan, and well he asked if I could go."

"Are Mr. and Mrs. Brown going?" William questioned.

Wrapping the dish towel around her hand and then unwrapping it and repeating the motion several times, she finally replied, "No. It would just be me and Georgie."

"What time should I be expecting you home tomorrow?"

No longer able to make eye contact with her father, staring at the floor she answered, "We would be spending the night at the cottage and coming home sometime the following day."

"Nope. Absolutely not. You are way too young to be spending the night with a boy."

Wilma threw the dish towel on the counter, "That's not fair. I'm seventeen years old. I'm practically an adult." she yelled.

"Adults don't throw fits like you are right now."

"But father please?" Wilma begged, stomping her foot on the linoleum floor, "It is not like I'm going to end up pregnant like my birth mom did when she was seventeen," She tried reasoning.

Holding firm to his parental decision, William calmly answered, "The answer is no and that's final. Now, please finish drying the dishes and put them away."

"I hate you!" his daughter tearfully screamed, grabbing a plate and smashing it into a million pieces. She ran up the stairs and slammed her door, shaking the entire house.

As William made his way up the stairs to his bedroom, Angela stepped out into the hallway tying up her blue bathrobe, "William darling, why don't you just let her go? It's the first summer you aren't dragging her to California. Let her have fun with her friends."

"Angela, she is just a child."

"She is seventeen years old William, almost eighteen."

"She is a child. I am her father and what I say goes. If you want to have a baby, Angela, you have to learn you can't let them do whatever they want," he said, trying hard not to lose his temper.

Angela stared at her husband, her anger almost at the boiling point, "Don't you ever tell

me I don't know anything about raising kids,"
She replied in an angry whisper before turning
back into the bedroom and slamming the door
in her husband's face.

William sighed as he banged his
forehead on the closed door, "Women," Then
he walked down the stairs. He poured himself
a glass of whiskey and took a long swig.

"Don't ever try to understand them. It will
only drive you insane," he heard his father call
as he stepped outside onto the porch and lit a
cigarette.

5

The next morning Wilma was buttering herself
some toast when a red 1958 Chevrolet Delray
made its way up the long gravel driveway.
When it stopped the driver honked the horn.
Wilma looked out the window and realized it

was Georgie. She quickly put the butter knife down and grabbed a silver platter off the counter and used it to check her reflection. Then she walked out onto the back porch.

"Morning, babe. Are you ready to go?" Georgie asked as he made his way out of the car.

"My dad won't let me go," Wilma scoffed.

Georgie made his way onto the porch and kissed Wilma, "Why not?"

"Because he is being a square at the moment. Thinks we are too young to be spending the night together."

"For real?" Georgie sighed, "Man the older you get, the tighter your pops is getting on those reins."

"I'm seventeen. When my birth mom was seventeen, she gave birth to me. Guess he thinks I'm going to end up with a bun in the oven too."

Leaning closer to Wilma, Gorgie whispered in her ear, "Won't have to worry about that. I packed protection, babe."

Wilma laughed and pushed him away, "What makes you think anything was going to happen, huh?"

Taking her hand in his, Georgie looked her in the eyes and smiled, "Well...I don't know. Guess I was maybe hoping...you know."

Just then the car door opened and a voice called out, "Hey are we going anytime soon, or am I going to have to wait until you two love birds get married?"

Wilma turned her glance towards the car. Her eyes became big and her temper started to boil when she saw Maryanne getting out of the car. She was wearing a tight black leather jumpsuit that accentuated all her curves. Her bright red lips held tight to a cigarette as she inhaled deeply, then she blew out little ringlets of smoke.

"What is she doing here!" Wilma demanded.

"Well, see babe, Maryanne and Davie were going to come with us, but since Davie got in that fight, his pops won't let him out of the house. So now it's just the three of us."

"I can't go!" she exclaimed, "REMEMBER?" She pronounced every syllable slowly in the word remember.

"She can't go," Georgie called to Maryanne.

"Aww, what's the matter? Little daddy's girl isn't allowed?" Maryanne taunted.

"You are not still going are you, Georgie?" Wilma angrily inquired.

"Well, yeah. Why wouldn't I?"

"Um, because I am your girlfriend and I can't go!"

"Well yeah, but..." Georgie stammered, "I have the car packed and I've had this trip planned for a month now."

"Come on Georgie. I'm waiting." Maryanne called.

"Look, babe, nothing will happen between me and Maryanne. I promise," Georgie replied as he kissed Wilma on the cheek and hurried to the car.

Wilma watched as Georgie and Maryanne disappeared down the gravel driveway in a cloud of dust. Then she ran inside and headed up the stairs to her bedroom. Her father followed, "Wilma, what is wrong?"

"I hate you. It's all your fault!" she screamed in her father's face before slamming her bedroom door.

Feeling defeated, William hung his head as he entered the dining room and joined his parents at the breakfast table.

"It's hard raising a teenage girl, son. And it's extremely hard for you as the only parent and a male, no doubt," his mother explained, "You have no idea what teenage girls go through."

"You have a wife," his father stated, "Let her help."

"But father, she doesn't have kids of her own. She doesn't have parenting experience."

"Oh my goodness son!" his mother scolded, "don't ever pass judgement like that on anyone, especially never on women. We know far more than you think."

"Believe me son, your mom is right," his father agreed, "Give Angela a chance and let her help."

William was quiet for a moment and then let his ego go, "Angela, darling," he called, "Will you please come in the dining room?"

"Yes dear, what do you need?" Angela asked as she wiped her wet, soapy hands on her apron.

William sighed and hung his head, "I think it's time I let go of the reins a bit. Wilma needs a woman in her life. And you're her step-mom. So…"

Angela could tell this was hard for her husband so she interrupted him, "Say no more, darling. I would be honored."

Thrilled that her husband was allowing her to finally help with Wilma, she took her apron off and made her way upstairs. When she arrived at Wilma's bedroom door, nerves shot through her body. She had no idea what she should say. She knew what she wanted to say, but would it help or just make the situation worse?

Gently knocking on the door and slowly opening it, she peeked her head inside, "Wilma, sweetie, can we talk?" When there was no answer, she opened the door fully and stepped inside, "Wilma?" she called out calmly. But no response came. She opened the closet door, but all that greeted her were Wilma's dresses. She quickly checked the other bedrooms upstairs but Wilma was nowhere to be found. Nervously, Angela ran back to Wilma's bedroom and froze when she noticed the window was open. She leaned her head out the window and instantly concluded that Wilma must have climbed down the tree and ran off.

6

Wilma hid in the horse barn behind bales of hay, staring at the cigarettes and bottle of whiskey she stole from the cabinet in her dad's bedroom. The tears flowed down her cheeks as she thought of Georgie and Maryanne alone in Georgie's cottage all weekend. Too preoccupied with her thoughts, she didn't hear when one of the ranch hands walked into the barn.

As the ranch hand put away his wheelbarrow and swept some bits of hay back into a horse stall, he thought he had heard someone cry out. At first glance the barn seemed empty, but as he walked towards the back by the hay bales, the crying and sniffling became more apparent. He followed the sound and found Wilma and the unopened bottle of whisky.

"Excuse me, miss. Is everything okay?"

"Leave me alone," Wilma uttered.

"I don't think I can leave you, not as long as you have that whiskey."

"You want to share it with me?" Wilma asked, wiping her nose on her arm.

"No," the ranch hand laughed, "but I know your father will be quite upset if you go back inside the house all sloshed."

"He probably wouldn't care. He only cares about himself."

"Oh, I doubt that."

"No it's true. If he cared about me, he would have let me go with Georgie. But now Georgie is doing who knows what with Maryanne. Well, it's Maryanne, so I can imagine what they are doing," Wilma said with disgust as tears rolled down her red cheeks.

"Hey don't cry," the ranch hand said as he knelt to Wilma's level, "I know your dad cares so much about you, that is why he wouldn't let you go. There is no need to cry over Georgie. Guys are so stupid. I should know, I am a guy."

This comment made Wilma laugh. She wiped the tears from her eyes and grabbed the whiskey bottle and sighed, "Guess you think I'm pretty square huh?"

"No, I think you are quite smart. If you wanted to have a drink or even a smoke just to piss your father off, you would have done it already."

"You know for a ranch hand you are pretty smart," Wilma chuckled.

"I know what it feels like to be in love and then have your heart broken."

Wilma stared at the ranch hand for a moment.

"I'm Franklin, but everyone calls me Franky," he said as he extended his hand towards Wilma.

"I'm Wilma. Everyone calls me...they call me Wilma," she replied as she shook Franky's hand.

Franky helped her to her feet and grabbed the whiskey bottle and cigarettes, "You and your father usually go to California during the summer don't you? Why not this summer?"

"How do you know that?"

"This is my third year helping your grandfather on the farm. I am in charge of all the guys here. Your grandfather tells me what needs to be done and I delegate the chores to everyone and help train the new guys. So why didn't you and your father take your annual trip."

"My dad always took me to California to search for my birth mom."

"You're adopted?" Franky asked, surprised.

"I don't know if you'd call it adopted really. My birth mom was young when she had me. Her father forced her to put me up for adoption the day I was born. I guess she wrote my dad who was stationed near the Philippians somewhere during the war," Wilma explained, "After he was discharged from the Navy, he came back to California and searched every orphanage until he found me and brought me here."

"See Wilma, your father cares and loves you very much. If he didn't, why would he have searched for you?"

"Wait," Wilma said, changing the subject and reaching her arm out to stop Franky from walking any further, "what are you planning on doing with those."

"Um, give them back to your father."

"Oh, hell no. I will get in so much trouble if he knows I took them. Quick, put them in my knapsack, I will sneak them back into his hiding spot later," Then Wilma ran back to the hay bales and hid her knapsack under the loose hay.

As she and Franky walked out of the barn they spotted her father and Angela running out of the house in a panic. When they spotted Wilma and Franky, they froze for an instant then ran to Wilma and hugged her and looked her over making sure she was okay.

"Stop. Stop touching me, I'm fine," Wilma begged and she tried to pull herself from her dad's embrace.

"I went up to your room. You weren't there," Angela breathed.

"I know I am your father, but if you ever need to talk...you know...about girl stuff...I want you to please come to me or Angela."

"Guys please, leave me alone. I'm fine," Wilma protested.

"Found her in the barn, sir. She's okay," Franky said as he shook William's hand.

"Thank you, son," William replied, shaking Franky's hand, "now back to work. Inside Wilma, we need to talk."

"Aww come on, Father, I'm fine, really I am." Wilma looked towards Angela for help.

"Don't smother her William, or she will never come to you for anything," Angela nudged.

Wilma nodded and smiled at Angela to thank her. Then, quickly checking behind her towards the barn, Wilma asked, "Um... can I help Franky with the chores today?"

William sighed but said, "As long as you don't get in his way, I guess you can."

With a big smile and a glint in her eyes, she thanked her father with a big hug and ran towards the barn, "Hey Franky wait up."

7

Saturday, June 5th, 1971

Dear Diary,

My dad didn't let me go with Georgie to Two
Rivers. He and Maryanne went though.. I
don't trust the hussy for anything. Georgie
and Maryanne swear up and down nothing
happened between them. He said she stayed
with some guys they met on the beach. Part
of me believes that story, but I still believe

Maryanne at least tried something with Georgie.

I still love Georgie, but I am kind of crushing on this other boy. He works on the farm for Grandpa. Franky is the head ranch hand. Dad has been letting me hang out in the barn with him as long as I don't get in Franky's way. Yesterday, Franky and I took the horses down to the stream. We carried on a conversation as though we've known each other forever. He was so easy to talk to and he didn't judge me and he laughed at my jokes. Georgie is taking me for ice cream tonight so I will end here.

The sunset was casting pink and purple hews over the bay as Georgie paid for his and

Wilma's chocolate swirl ice cream cones. They walked hand in hand to their favorite little spot on the rocks and let the waves crash over their bare feet as they ate their ice cream. The calls from the seagulls above blocked out any noise coming from all the tourists on the boardwalk.

"Any idea about what college you might attend once we graduate?" Georgie asked as he caught some melting ice cream with his tongue.

"My grade point average is high enough to attend the university in Oshkosh," Wilma replied, "I will probably get a teaching degree. How about you?"

"Oshkosh sounds good. Thinking I could go into agriculture or business, you know, something that will help when your gramps retires and gives us the farm."

"Gives us the farm?" Wilma coughed, getting caught off guard.

"Most farms are kept in the family, right? And since you are the only grandchild, Wilma, it only makes sense that after we get married, your gramps would want us to have the farm then we give it to our children someday."

Wilma laughed, "It seems like you are getting a little ahead of yourself Georgie."

"No, I'm not. I am what people call practical and thinking about the future," he said, sounding hurt, "I thought you wanted to get married."

"Well, I do. But we have not even graduated yet. Why rush things?"

Feeling frustrated, Georgie answered with a sigh, "Nevermind."

The couple finished their ice cream in awkward silence. Darkness had fallen over the town and the street lights came on casting wide paths for those on the boardwalk.

Wilma wiped her sticky hands on her skirt then hopped on Georgie's lap and hugged him tight, "Come on Georgie don't be mad. I honestly didn't mean to hurt your feelings."

"It's okay. I am over it," He replied, hugging her back. As his lips gently caressed hers, one of his hands held her back as the other slowly rubbed her smooth legs and made its way to her thigh.

Wilma giggled as she pushed his hand away from her thigh. She was thrilled she and

Georgie were being intimate like this. They hadn't been this close since before the summer started. Suddenly, she felt goosebumps on her arms as Georgie's lips made their way down her neck. He chuckled as she flinched. Georgie knew she was ticklish on her neck. Once again, his hand made its way up her thigh. And once again, Wilma pushed it away.

"Come on, Georgie, Let's go play ring toss and maybe get some cotton candy," She said as she stood up and helped Georgie to his feet.

The boardwalk was crowded with people. Mostly tourists who were staying at the nearby campgrounds or those who had summer cottages on the bay. Loud music and hoots and hollering rang out from a few bars full of drunk vacationers. Children, holding tight to balloon animals, ran to and fro as their parents chased behind them. Bells dinged and bright lights flashed from what few carnival games called the boardwalk home. The smell of fried food and cigarette smoke wafted in the air. Since Wilma spent every summer traveling to California, she was excited to take in all the sights and sounds the boardwalk had to offer that evening.

As Wilma and Georgie tossed red and yellow rings around bowling pins, they would hip bump one another to make the other miss the bowling pin. Everything was perfect in Wilma's mind until she heard the irritating voice of her former best friend.

"Ooh, Georgie. Hi, how are you?" Maryanne giggled as she purposely pushed Wilma out of the way and hugged Georgie.

"Hi, Maryanne. It's nice to see you too," he said as he uncomfortably returned her hug.

"What are you playing? I want to play too." She said as she grabbed a set of rings from the carny.

"Excuse me, Maryanne, can't you see that we are on a date?" Wilma said aggressively with her hands on her hips and her gaze piercing into Maryanne's soul.

"Oh, Georgie won't mind if I tag along. Will you Georgie?" Maryanne giggled as she jokingly hip-checked Georgie.

Wilma looked at Georgie for help, but he seemed speechless. Then Wilma went and sat down on a picnic table and watched helplessly as Maryanne forced hugs upon Georgie and purposely dropped a ring and bent down slowly to pick it up. When she missed a pin, she did a sexy pout with her lips and batted her long eyelashes at Georgie. When Maryanne was bored of ring toss, she grabbed Georgie's hand and dragged him to the Balloon Pop booth. Georgie glanced at Wilma and moved his shoulders up and down like he didn't know what to say or do. He pulled money out of his pocket and paid the carny for some darts.

Wilma was fuming. How dare that floozie take over her date like that. She had had enough of this. Wilma stood up from the picnic table and straightened her blue skirt that hung right above her knee. She tightened her ponytail and slipped off her sandals and let her feet feel the coolness of the grass for a minute while she thought of a plan.

"Hey Maryanne," Wima shouted as she pushed her way through the crowd, "Get your filthy paws off of my man!"

Maryanne turned and looked at Wilma, "What are you talking about?" she scoffed.

"You ruined my weekend away with Georgie and now you are ruining my date."

A crowd was gathering around the two girls, "It's not my fault your daddy wouldn't let you go with your boyfriend. Was he afraid you would lose your virginity?" Maryanne smirked.

Wilma could feel the anger bubbling up inside her body. She took a deep breath and then surprised herself when she said, "At least I don't have to spread my legs open to get a boy to like me," Then she took the sandals she was holding in her hand and smacked them across Maryanne's face. The adrenalin raced through her blood as she grabbed Georgie by the hand and ran quickly through the crowded boardwalk until they made it back to Georgie's car.

They sat in the car as Georgie fumbled for his keys, "Oh man, that was outta sight. I have never seen girls fight before." Georgie said excitedly.

"Would you just shut up and drive Georgie."

The ten minute drive back to the farm was quiet and awkward. Wilma was so mad at

Georgie. Why did he have to be so nice to everybody? How come he could tell her no, but he could never say no to anyone else? She was so mad at herself. She knew Maryanne didn't have the best home life. When they were younger, Maryanne spent the night quite a bit at her house because she was afraid to be around her parents when they were drinking. And now her best friend was finding comfort in men. Men that were only nice to her until they were tired of her.

Wilma was so lost in her thoughts, she did not realize Georgie had driven up her driveway and was now holding the car door open for her.

"You amaze me Wilma," he said as he helped her out of the car.

"I know." Wilma sighed as Georgie kissed her on the cheek.

"Get some sleep and we will talk tomorrow okay," he smiled, kissing the back of her soft hand before he got back in the car and drove away.

8

Wilma sat on the rope swing hanging from the oak tree outside her bedroom window. Her hands held loosely the braided polyester rope that held the seat made of old barn wood. It once was painted a deep red, but now weathered with curls of peeling paint.

Songs from the crickets and bullfrogs filled the late summer night. The coyotes added to the melody, as they cried out to the full moon. Stars twinkled brightly above as though God himself tossed diamond dust over the earth. The country on a summer night was magnificent.

Wilma thought about the events that transpired on the boardwalk that night. Lost in her thoughts, she didn't hear Franky walk up behind her.

"Evening," He said as he leaned against the oak tree. The moon so bright, Wilma could see a twinkle in his eyes.

"You scared me," Wilma chuckled.

"I didn't mean to. Are you okay? You seem...lost."

Wilma told Franky about her date with Georgie. She told him how Maryanne barged her way in and then told him about the argument and slapping Maryanne with her sandals.

"Wow, I am sorry I missed that," Franky laughed, "You know what you need?" he said as he twisted the rope swing and held it smiling into Wilma's eyes.

"What?" she asked as she prepared for what was coming next.

"You need to forget about Maryanne and Georgie, and start having some fun in your life," Franky answered, and then he let go of the twisted up swing and watched as Wilma spun around and around.

When the swing had stopped spinning, Wilma got up and tried to run after Franky. Laughing and dizzy, she tripped over her own feet and fell into the damp dew covered grass.

Fanky followed and fell beside her, both laughing until their insides hurt.

Once the world stopped spinning, Wilma said, "Thanks. I needed a good laugh."

"Glad I could help," Franky replied, smiling up at the stars.

The two friends talked about the constellations and talked about how life would forever be changed if people could walk on the moon. They joked about how the moon might taste like swiss cheese, and if it would fall apart like a cookie dipped in milk. At times, they would just lay silent, and listen to what nature had to offer them that summer night.

After a while, Franky sat up and stretched, "I should probably get going. I'm sure it's after midnight."

"Agreed," Wilma replied with a yawn.

As they made their way to their feet, their heads collided.

"Oh, I'm sorry are you okay?" Wilma asked, rubbing her forehead.

"Of course. No worries," Franky answered, rubbing his head.

Then their eyes met and froze, almost as if asking for permission for what came next. In an instant, Wilma moved her face closer to Franky's. Their lips met and locked in a spontaneous kiss that sent a warm fuzzy feeling though Wilma's entire body. As quickly as it happened, it ended. Both a little surprised and nervous.

"Oh, my gosh, I'm sorry I should not have done that," Wilma apologized.

"No, it was my fault. I apologize." Franky grinned.

"I...um..thought it was nice." Wilma whispered, staring at the ground.

"Me too," Franky replied, lifting Wilma's chin with his finger. He kissed her again with more passion.

9

Dear Diary,

These last two weeks have been confusing. I want to tell Georgie about Franky's kiss, but I know it would hurt him. I feel bad I am pushing him away. Every time I catch Franky looking at me, I feel a smile across my lips and my stomach fills with butterflies. The other night we snuck out into the blueberry patch and made out under the stars. He is such a great kisser. I just don't know what to do. Franky left early this morning. His parents are going on vacation up to Rhode Island and wanted him to go along. Georgie and I are going to the dance *tonight. It will be nice to just focus on each other for once. But what I would like is a vacation away from both boys.*

The rec center was all abuzz when Georgie and Wilma arrived. In the large, dim room, a rainbow of balloons hovered in the middle of the dance floor. White and yellow crepe paper was intricately hung on the walls and on the stage where Georgie's mom stood, placing another vinyl on the turntable and gently placing the needle down. The young ladies in their summer dresses and fresh pixie haircuts gathered on the dance floor. Fellas in crisp white t-shirts and jeans with leather jackets and slicked-back hair followed as Elvis Presley's *Jailhouse Rock* came through the speakers.

"Come on babe, let's boogie," Georgie said excitedly as he grabbed Wilma's hand and led her onto the dance floor.

An array of colored skirts flared up as the guys twirled their ladies around the dance floor. Hips were gyrating as the guys tried impersonating Elvis. The chaperons were separating dancers who were getting too close for the church lady's comfort. And then, of course, their bodies would reunite in passion once the chaperon was out of sight.

Everyone clapped politely when the song ended, waiting patiently as Georgie's mom put on another record. A giant circle formed on the floor as Chubby Checker started belting out the words to *The Twist*. Bodies were twisting up and down and all around. Couples would take turns in the middle of the circle twisting and thrusting their bodies until another brave couple would jump in the middle.

The next record was a slow song. The ladies grabbed their beaus and placed their heads ever so sweetly upon his shoulder as they swayed to the melody.

"Oh Georgie, let's slow dance."

"Yeah right, not with my mom here watching us," Georgie muttered.

"Come on. What is so wrong about your mom being here watching?"

"Nothing. It's just that we can't be us if you know what I mean."

Getting frustrated, Wilma replied, "No I don't know what you mean. I want to slow dance," she demanded as she started to walk away.

"Come on, babe, don't be like this," Georgie begged as he grabbed her arm, "You're going to make a scene."

"Just how am I going to make a scene?" Wilma demanded, stomping her heeled shoe hard on the linoleum.

William wrapped one arm around her waist and pulled her closer to himself. Gently he whispered in her ear, "Look around, Wilma. Look how all the couples are cuddling, swaying back and forth."

"Yeah, I see that. So why can't we be like those couples?"

"Because my mom and the other chaperones are coming around pulling those couples apart because they are getting too close for comfort. I want to be close to you. Uninterrupted closeness, Wilma."

Wilma looked into Georgie's. Sighing, she gave in. "Oh, alright Georgie, let's go get some punch."

Some of the fellas who didn't have dates were gathered around the punch bowl shouting catcalls to some of the couples on the dance floor.

"Hey, Georgie, what are you and your old lady up to tonight? Y'all want to cut out? This dance is such a drag. We're going to try and score some sixers and hang at the park tonight. You in?"

Georgie gave Wilma a hopeful look but she just glared back. He already knew her answer.

One of the fellas handed Wilma and Georgie cups of punch.

"Hey, guys, try this. We had to do something to liven up this shindig," he laughed.

Wilma and Georgie along with some of the other fellas started to drink the punch. Then Wilma spat it out with a loud wail, "This punch tastes awful."

All the guys started laughing and punching each other in the arm.

"That's right. We spiked it," one laughed as he drew his jacket aside and showed Georgie the bottle of vodka.

Then one of the guys noticed two of the chaperons looking in the direction of the punch table and one started to make her way over.

"Alright fellas, let's scat. Meet us at the park Georgie," one ordered as the group headed for the door.

"Georgie I don't want to hang with them. I thought we were on a date!" Wilma exclaimed as she crossed her arms over her chest and tapped her foot waiting for him to explain.

Feeling a little disappointed, Georgie reluctantly agreed with Wilma and gave her a soft peck on the cheek.

"How about we grab a burger and fries at the Third Street Diner and skip the park?"

"Sounds wonderful, Georgie."

It was quiet in the diner. An elderly couple sat in a booth near the counter sipping on their decaf coffee as a waitress in a pink pinstripe outfit cleared plates from their table. Two older gentlemen sat at the counter smoking cigars and conversed about how this year's crops were going to fair. Georgie nodded at two teenagers he recognized from school in a booth in the back corner as he and Wilma sat in a booth in the opposite corner. The same waitress who cleared the elderly couple's table followed behind them with two glasses of water and menus.

As Wilma glanced at the menu Georgie mustered up the courage and said, " Wilma, I have some news."

"What?"

"Well, I'm going down to the city to look at apartments next week and I want you to accompany me."

Wilma put the menu down and stared at Georgie.

"You know my dad won't let me go. Don't you remember, he didn't let me go with you to the cottage."

"Yes, but my folks will be coming this time."

"Wait, why are you going apartment hunting?"

Georgie reached into his leather jacket and pulled out a folded envelope and handed it to Wilma.

"I didn't want to mention anything until it was official, but I have an early acceptance into business school. I just have to finish the first semester of our senior year."

Wilma read over the letter carefully.

"Are you two ready to order?" Asked a gum smacking-waitress. Her pinstripe uniform was the same shade of pink as her gum.

"Well," Wilma said with an unsure smile, "This calls for a celebration. A double, hot fudge sundae with two cherries please," she paused for a moment then asked, "Georgie, what are you going to have?"

"Two spoons, please." he chuckled, "Wilma, I want you to accompany me because I want you to like the apartment. I want you to be comfortable there. It's going to be yours too."

"What do you mean, *mine too*?"

The waitress placed the double fudge sundae with two cherries on top in front of the couple. Georgie took a small spoonful and placed it ever so gently in Wilma's mouth, then enthusiastically announcing, "Marry me, Wilma!"

Wilma choked on the spoonful of ice cream, coughing loud enough to get the attention of the two gentlemen at the counter.

"Marry you? Now?" she stammered.

"No, not now. At the end of the first semester. When I'm done with school."

"But Georgie, I have to finish school. We can't get married."

"I know that's silly. And I want you to finish school. You will just be a married woman when you graduate. Besides, Travis and Linda are getting married next week. They are going to be seniors just like us."

"They are getting married because Travis is going off to Vietnam," Wilma implied, "You will be going off to school. There's a difference you know."

Georgie placed his hands around Wilma's, "Think about it, please. I love you Wilma and I want to spend the rest of my life with you."

Wilma looked into his eyes and smiled, "I will think about it."

When the couple arrived back at Wilma's house, Georgie opened her car door and helped her out. Instead of heading for the house, Wilma led him into the barn, past the horses, and into the hayloft. The moonlight shone brightly through the cracks of the barn wall. The smell of fresh hay filled their noses as a horse neighed gently. Wilma pushed Georgie up against a stack of hay bales. Her warm mouth pressed up against his. Georgie's hands made their way up the back of her blouse. Then Wilma pushed away from him.

"I need to know if you slept with Maryanne."

"Of course I didn't. Why would you think that Wilma?" Georgie asked, feeling insulted.

"Well...It's just that she went away with you to your cottage that first weekend of this summer. And she was all over you at the boardwalk. So it has crossed my mind."

"You know how Maryanne is Wilma. Once she saw all the shirtless guys on the beach at my cottage, I didn't see her for the rest of the weekend. And her actions on the boardwalk, well...she may just be jealous of you."

"Of me?" Wilma asked, surprised, "Why me?"

"You have a wonderful home life. You have a handsome boyfriend, and look at you! My goodness, you are gorgeous," Georgie answered as he leaned in and kissed her neck.

For Wilma, that was all she needed to hear. She unbuttoned her blouse and let it fall off her arms onto the hay. Then she unbuttoned her skirt and let that fall too. She stood in front of her boyfriend, the boy who a few hours earlier, asked her to marry him. She still had to think about marriage, but for now, she knew she wanted to be with Georgie.

10

Dear Diary,

I can't believe so much has happened in just a week. Georgie proposed to me and we did "IT" three times. I feel so alive, so grown up, so...so like a woman. I do wish Maryanne and I were still friends. I really want to tell someone. As for his proposal, I haven't answered him yet. So many things I am unsure of and plus we still have our entire senior year of high school ahead of us. Franky is coming back to the farm after his family vacation to Rhode Island. I am excited to see him and hear all about his trip.

Wilma was locking the little padlock on her diary and was carefully hiding it under her mattress when she heard a tap on her second-story window. She stared at the window waiting to hear the tap again. Then came a second and a third tap. She cautiously walked to the window and peered out. Standing by the big oak tree was Franky, winding up his arm to throw another stone at the window. Wilma quickly opened up the window.

"Hi Franky," she called, "I'll be right down." She stopped in front of her mirror and touched her hair up a bit, smoothed lip gloss over her lips, and ran down the stairs and into Franky's arms.

"Hi, Wilma, how are you?" He asked as he kissed her on the lips and twirled her around.

"I am good. How was your trip? I can't wait to hear all about it!" Wilma cheerfully exclaimed as she hugged Franky.

"This evening, after I finish here at the farm, it will be just you and me. Maybe we can take the horses down to the stream."

"Oh Franky, that will be absolutely divine. I'll pack us dinner in the picnic basket."

Wilma spent the day doing her chores around the house and outside in the garden. Her grandmother often asked what she was daydreaming about, as Wilma would hang clothes haphazardly on the clothesline or put clean dishes in the wrong cupboard. Wilma would simply say she wasn't daydreaming, she was just happy and enjoying the warm summer weather.

That evening, while the family ate their supper, Wilma pushed her food from one side of the plate to the other with her fork. When she thought no one was looking, she would carefully put her food in her napkin. When her plate was empty and her napkin full, she quickly jumped up and offered to wash everyone's plates. She wrapped the food from the napkin in tinfoil. She grabbed two glass bottles of Pepsi and a bottle opener and placed them in the picnic basket along with the tin foiled food. She grabbed the silver platter that was sitting on the counter and checked her reflection.

As she was making her way to the back porch, the phone rang.

"Wilma, can you answer that please?" Her father shouted from the dining room.

Hurriedly, she picked up the receiver and quickly answered, "Barret residence, Wilma speaking."

The voice on the other end came through, "Hiya, Wilma, it's me, Georgie."

Caught completely off guard, Wilma stammered, "Georgie, hi."

"Listen," he said, "We got home from the city late this afternoon. I found an apartment I think you would like. Can I come over and tell you all about it?"

Wilma stood frozen for a minute, not sure what to say, "Um... Georgie, not tonight. I...um...have a bad headache. I um...just want to lay down and sleep."

"Oh, well, I could come over and make you some soup or rub your head so you feel better."

"Georgie, not tonight. Maybe you could come over tomorrow. I have to go now. Bye," and she hung the receiver back on the wall. Her heart was pounding fast. She couldn't believe she had just lied to Georgie. She felt a little guilty as she made her way outside and down the porch towards the barn.

The instant she saw Franky saddling the horses, her guilt had morphed into excitement. His arm muscles flexed as he lifted the brown leather saddles onto her horses, Peppermint and Chestnut. They stood calmly as Franky pulled the straps through the buckles. He was so gentle with the horses, patting each of them on their muzzle before checking their hooves. Before he grabbed the reins and led them out of the stable, Franky pulled a red bandana out of his back jean pocket. He took his cowboy hat off and wiped the sweat from his brow. That warm fuzzy feeling shot through Wilma's body again. She couldn't help but wonder what it would have been like if she had lost her virginity to Franky instead of Georgie.

Daydreaming once again, Wilma didn't hear Franky say her name as he led the horses out of the barn. Once Peppermint nudged her with his velvety muzzle Wilma blinked and smiled at Franky.

"You must be thinking awfully hard about something," he laughed as he took the small picnic basket from her and strapped it onto Chestnut.

"I'm just happy to see you, that's all," Wilma replied with a smile.

"I can tell," Franky said as he wrapped his arms around her waist and kissed her passionately on her mouth. Then he helped her mount Peppermint before he mounted Chestnut. "Come on, let's see whatcha got," he said as they took off racing through the field.

At the edge of the field, the couple pulled Peppermint and Chestnut to a halt. "I win," Wilma proudly announced as she patted Peppermint on his neck.

"How long have you been riding?" Franky asked as he tried to steady Chestnut.

"All my life, I guess. And you?" Wilma asked as she eyed Franky and laughed at his uncomfortableness upon Chestnut.

"Three years maybe. Your grandfather sort of taught me. He said if I have to work with the horses, I need to ride horses too. I think I would enjoy the horses better when my feet are on the ground."

Wilma laughed, "You're doing just fine, cowboy. Come on, I want to show you something."

The horses cantered through the woods and up a path to the top of the hill. Looking down into the valley, they could see the farm and the gravel driveway that wound its way to the main road into town. Further in the distance the bay melted into the horizon as the setting sun cast pink and purple hues onto the water. The huge fishing boats making their way home for the night, turned into small black specks, moving at a snail's pace.

"It's so peaceful up here," Franky said, breaking the silence.

"I know. This is my favorite spot in the world. Peppermint and I used to come up here all the time."

"Do you ever bring Georgie up here?"

Wilma gave Franky a puzzling look, then replied, "No. Georgie is a working, book reading type of boy. He is uncomfortable around the horses and even the little chickens," Wilma chuckled, "He's going to business school after the first semester. He has it in his head that my dad will someday sell him the farm."

Franky climbed off Chestnut and tied the reins to a birch tree.

"I thought we were going down to the creek?" Wilma asked.

"The view from here is amazing. Let's picnic here," Franky answered, as he took Peppermint's reins and tied them to the tree.

Wilma untied the picnic basket from the horse as Franky spread a saddle blanket on the ground for them to dine on. Franky told Wilma all about the magnificent mansions of Newport, Rhode Island. He told her how he and his family flew kites at Brenton Point State Park, and how he lost his kite over the big rocks where the Narragansett Bay meets the Atlantic Ocean. He explained how his mom thought a certain Bed and Breakfast on the popular Thames Street was so elegant, and that when his dad retires she wants to open one just like it. He even told Wilma about St. Mary's Catholic Church and how President Kennedy and his wife were married there only a few years ago.

Wilma listened with great intent as Franky talked about his trip. She loved the way his eyes twinkled with excitement and how he used his hands and arms so enthusiastically throughout his story. By the time Franky had finished, the sun had completely sunk below the bay. Crickets chirped and an owl in the distance made its presence known.

"Oh dear, we better head back. I don't want my dad and Angela to worry. I don't think I even told them that I was taking the horses out," Wilma said as she scrambled to gather their things in the dark.

"They know. I spoke with your dad earlier today. Told him we may go riding for a bit after I was done with the barn," Franky reassured Wilma, "But I agree, we should head back."

By the light of the moon, the horses made their way down the hill, across the field and back into the barn. Wilma helped Franky take the saddles off, check the horses' hooves and throw in a bale of hay before closing up the barn for the night.

"I had a really nice time tonight Franky."

"I as well," he replied, taking her hands in his, "Can I see you tomorrow?"

Wilma sighed, "Um, Georgie wants to come over tomorrow."

"I take it you two are getting along now?" Franky questioned.

"I don't know. I guess," Wilma answered, not sure if she wanted to tell Franky more.

He looked into her eyes and saw the reflection of the moon, "Wilma, I really like you. I could never break your heart the way Georgie has this summer. You deserve someone so much better than Georgie."

Wilma looked at the ground and watched her foot twist in the soft, dry dirt. Looking up she replied, "I really like you to Franky. I...I just have a lot to think about."

"Take your time," he said sweetly in her ear before kissing her on the cheek, "but not too much time, okay?" He smiled and walked to his blue 1959 Chevy pickup truck. He blew her a kiss before driving down the gravel driveway.

11

The next morning Wilma came bounding down the stairs, poured a glass of orange juice, and walked into the dining room.

"We are so excited for you Wilma," Angela said as she gave Wilma a hug before heading into the kitchen.

"We do have some things to discuss, but we might be able to work something out," her father said as he wiped his mouth with a napkin.

"We are so proud of the young lady you have grown into," her grandmother cheered as she carried plates into the kitchen.

Confused and not quite awake, Wilma asked, "What are you guys talking about?"

"Georgie here has been telling us he has an early acceptance into business school. He was apartment hunting this past weekend. Wilma why didn't you say anything?"

Shocked, Wilma stuttered, "Well...I...um."

"Oh Wilma, you are going to make a beautiful bride," Angela cheered as she came behind Wilma and twisted up her long strawberry blonde hair. "You and I will have so much fun shopping for your dress."

"Excuse me, I think I should have a say in this, don't you think?" Wilma demanded as she set her glass of orange juice on the table. "Georgie, I told you I wanted to think about all of this first. I did not accept your proposal," she announced as she glared at Georgie.

"As the man of this house and family, I think I have the right to say something," Grandpa announced as he pushed his chair back and rose up with both of his hands clutching the buckles of his overalls, "Wilma is only seventeen years old. She has not even started her senior year of high school yet. Let the girl live a little and stop suffocating her."

"Thank you, Grandpa," Wilma leaned over and kissed him on his whiskery cheek. "Georgie, let's go talk outside."

The early July morning was already a scorcher. Heatwaves glistened off the ground in the distance. The barnyard animals were already seeking shade from the morning sun.

Most of the ranch hands were shirtless and sweaty as they did their morning chores. Wilma caught a glimpse of Franky hopping off the tractor he was working on. Yesterday, Grandpa had mentioned it needed new spark plugs. Franky looked towards the porch and tipped his hat towards Wilma. She did a little wave, hoping Georgie didn't see.

"I apologize, Wilma. I didn't mean to tell your pops about my proposal. I was just so excited about school and the apartment. I think you're really going to like it. It has an outdoor pool that is just for residences. The back porch overlooks this big park where kids play football and baseball on the weekends. And it has an elevator so you won't have to carry groceries up three flights of stairs."

Wilma stood up from the porch swing, walked over to the railing, and leaned her back up against it. Crossing her arms she faced Georgie and asked, "What if I want to go to college and make something of myself?"

Georgie stood up and walked over to her. He placed his hands on her hips and leaned in and placed his forehead on hers,

"Baby, you can do whatever your heart desires, unless we start our family right away."

Wilma pushed him off of her before he could kiss her, "Look, Georgie, I need time to think about things. I think you should leave now before I tell you what's really on my mind."

"I respect your decision, and again, I apologize Wilma," he said as his soft lips grazed the back of her hand. "I will see you tonight for the fireworks your pops is shooting off," he said as he walked down the steps to his car.

Wilma watched as Georgie drove away in a cloud of gravel dust. Angela came out with two glasses of ice-cold lemonade. Handing one to Wilma, she asked, "Everything okay?"

Wilma sighed as she sat down, "Have you ever been in love with two boys at the same time?"

"Oh, this sounds serious," Angela said as she plopped down on the swing next to Wilma, "Is the other boy cute like Georgie? Is he a good kisser? Who is it?"

"Angela, please. I need advice from an adult, not some giddy school girl."

"Yes, you're right. I'm sorry Wilma," Angela apologized as she fixed her skirt, crossed her legs, and looked intently at Wilma. With pursed lips she said encouragingly, "please...continue."

Wilma couldn't help but laugh at her stepmom. She had never truly been fond of Angela, but right now she really needed a woman closer in age than her grandma to talk with.

"Georgie is wonderful, yes, but this other guy...well, he is so different from Georgie. Like Georgie, he is a hard worker. But unlike Georgie, he makes me laugh all the time, he enjoys the same things I do. And we have a lot of fun together."

"You and Georgie have been together for about nine months, right?"

"Yeah."

"So tell me what you like about Georgie."

"Well, he is a hard worker, well educated, he has his future planned out and he wants me in it," Wilma paused for a moment.

"You have been with him for nine months and that's all you got out of the relationship?" Angela questioned.

"No. I mean, we used to have a lot of fun together. We took romantic walks on the beach and had fun dates on the boardwalk. I love how he calls me when he gets off from work, he phones me to tell me he loves me and he can't wait to see me the next day. He gives me flowers and writes me little love notes and kisses my hand like a gentleman. There was a time wherein my mind, I couldn't wait to marry Georgie. But now...now that he actually sort of proposed, I...I just don't know anymore."

Angela pondered for a moment, "So how has this other fella made your relationship with Georgie difficult?"

"He hasn't. He knows Georgie and I are dating. But the more time I spend with this guy, the more I like him. He is so kind to the farm animals and…"

"Wait, he's a ranch hand?"

"Yes. What's wrong with ranch hands?

"Nothing. Continue."

"I was watching him get the horses ready before we took them out yesterday. He knows his way around them and he is so gentle with them. He isn't too keen on riding but he'll get used to it. And he wants me to be me, and to be happy. He isn't too fond of the way Georgie has been treating me this summer. And he makes my stomach get full of butterflies when we...kiss," Wilma replied with a big smile. "When Georgie and I kiss, I don't feel the butterflies like I used to."

"It sounds like you have it bad for this cowboy of yours. You haven't...um...slept with him have you, Wilma?" Angela inquired softly.

Wilma stared at her feet and tangled her fingers together nervously, "No," she whispered.

"You and Georgie havent...you know," Angela inquired nervously.

Wilma didn't respond.

"Oh Wilma," Angela said, disappointed, "You didn't. Please tell me you didn't."

"Yes, but only three times. Please don't tell my father," she begged.

"Does your cute ranch hand know you and Georgie have slept together?"

Wilma shook her head no.

"Did you at least use protection?"

"Of course, we aren't stupid," Wilma retorted.

The two sat quietly on the porch swing. Wilma was too embarrassed and confused to say anything. Angela was wondering if she should tell her husband and what steps she should take next.

"You know Wilma, I haven't seen my Aunt Carol and Uncle John since your father and I got married. Maybe the three of us could take a trip some time soon to visit them. They don't live far from our state capital. Maybe we could tour the Capitol. There is also this eccentric house built on a rock that just opened last summer for tours. Maybe if you get away from here you will be able to clear your head for a bit."

"A little vacation might just be what I need," Wilma agreed as she gave Angela a hug. "Please don't tell my father about...you know."

That night, holes were dug in the ground and filled with burning split hickory wood. Racks were assembled above the pits lined with chicken smothered in bar-b-q sauce. Big cast iron pots were placed upon other fire pits boiling corn on the cob. Franky and all of the ranch hands were invited to stay for dinner and participate in Grandpa's annual Fourth of July baseball game.

Georgie set up the picnic tables and lawn chairs and helped Wilma carry out the different potato salads and pies Grandma made earlier in the day.

After everyone had indulged in the bountiful dinner and darkness had crept into the valley, Grandpa delighted in lighting off his fireworks display. The loud booms from the explosions echoed off the hills, as the dark sky filled with reds, whites, and blues. One of the ranch hands strummed his guitar and serenaded everyone with the latest Elvis Presley song.

Georgie and Wilma lay on their backs watching the sky light up.
From time to time, Georgie would pop up and steal a kiss and then tickle Wilma.

"You look beautiful tonight," He whispered, as he went in for a more passionate kiss.

"Thank you."

"There is a small get together tonight on the bay. We have been invited. What do you say?"

"You know those types of get-togethers aren't my thing. The fuzz always seems to break them up. Besides, you don't want to do anything that will jeopardize your future."

"Aww, come on Wilma, it's summertime. You need to live a little."

Wilma sat up and looked Georgie in the eyes, "If you want to marry me, Georgie, you need to grow up a bit."

"Wait, are you finally saying yes to my proposal?" he asked hopeful.

"No, I didn't say that. I just don't want my husband thinking he can go galavanting all over whenever he wants. There is a fine line between a boy and manhood."

"How about this? Why don't we go? Just this one last time. You know, just to get the galavanting out of our systems."

12

He opened them with a bottle opener from his key ring and handed one to Wilma. They sat in the cool sand as they listened to one guy exaggerate a rumble he was in with some guy at the dinner. It was thAs Wilma and Georgie arrived on the beach, the stars twinkled above as the moonlight reflected off the bay. Fireworks echoed and illuminated the sky from the surrounding towns. Just about everyone who was anyone was at the fourth of July beach party. Between two piers was a huge bonfire. People gathered around and told the latest stories of their fishing trips and how lame their summer jobs had become while throwing back a six-pack. Just down from the bonfire, people were taking down the net as it was now too dark for a game of badminton.

Georgie grabbed two ice-cold bottles of beer out of an ice chest. He and Wilma sat on the cool sand and listened to music from a transistor radio as people danced all around them.

When the couple finished their beer, Georgie grabbed two more from an ice chest and headed for the next bonfire as the tunes from the transistor softly faded into the night air. Georgie held Wilma's hand to make sure she wouldn't stray too far. Once the second beer touched her lips, she became a little goofy and would stumble through the sand. Wilma was not much of a drinker and it quickly became apparent to Georgie.

The hiccups set in as Wilma felt a gentle tap on her right shoulder. She turned around and was face to face with Maryanne.

"Hiya, Maryanne," she said most cheerfully as she hiccuped.

"Hiya back," Maryanne replied as she took a long drag from her cigarette and exhaled the smoke in Wilma's direction. "So I hear you and Georgie are getting hitched soon."

Wilma looked around for Georgie and saw him standing with some guys from school. She hiccuped again, "I haven't said yes yet. I have a lot to think about."

"You know you will say yes. You have been planning your wedding since you and he started dating. I bet he only proposed to you so he could get you in bed."

"Why don't you just shut your filthy mouth, Maryanne," Wilma exclaimed as she took Maryanne's cigarette out of her hand and jammed it into her beer bottle.

"I'm just sorry I'm not going to be here to see the wedding of the decade," Maryanne scoffed as she took another cigarette out of her black clutch she had tucked under her arm.

"Who said you will be invited?"

"You don't have to get your panties all in a bunch," Maryanne laughed, "I really just came to tell you bye. My folks are shipping me out of town for a few months."

"Your parents must be so excited," Wilma replied sarcastically as she turned and looked for Georgie.

In a somber tone, Maryanne asked, "Don't you want to know why I'm leaving?"

"Not really. Now if you will excuse me, I need to find Georgie."

"I know what people are saying about me. And I used to not care. Most of what people know about me is lies. Most guys make up stuff about me just to impress their friends. I should have stopped the lies when they first started. At first, I liked the attention I was receiving," Maryanne paused to wipe a tear from her cheek, "Then one night, me and one of our friends had just a bit too much to drink. And then...and then..." Maryanne sobbed as tears rolled down her cheeks.

"Oh my goodness, were you forced into sex?" Wilma whispered.

"No, I agreed to do it. I wanted to do it. I was angry and I thought getting revenge would make me feel better."

Wilma looked baffled. She was silent for a minute before whispering, "Are you pregnant?"

Maryanne sobbed harder as she shook her head up and down. Wilma gave her old friend a tight hug and stroked her hair, reassuring her all would be okay.

"I'm so sorry, Wilma, I didn't mean for this to happen."

Wilma released her grip from Maryanne and chuckled, "You don't have to apologize to me. You should be apologizing to your folks."

"No, I can't leave until you know I'm truly sorry. You don't have to forgive me, but I want you to know I didn't mean for this to happen."

Wilma chuckled again, "You're making it sound like Georgie got you pregnant." The second it came out of her mouth she froze and terror flooded her eyes as she stared at Maryanne with disbelief, " It was only a month ago when you and he went to his cabin. You wouldn't know if you were pregnant yet. He promised me he didn't touch you. He said you went and spent the entire weekend with some guy you met on the beach," Wilma yelled, getting the attention of everyone on the beach.

"Hey, what's all the yelling about girls?" Georgie slurred as he stumbled through the sand.

"Is everything okay, Wilma?" Franky asked as he put his arm around her.

"You are just evil and jealous of me Maryanne. I always had everything so much easier than you did. I supported you. I helped you and let you stay at my house when things got rough at yours. And now, after all these years of friendship, you go and make up a horrible lie about Georgie. Why, Maryanne, why?" Wilma screamed, "Take me home, Franky. I don't want to be here anymore."

Darkness surrounded the truck as Franky drove further and further from town. The silence was broken by the soothing sound of the truck's engine. Wilma was so angry, her adrenaline kept her from crying.

Franky turned the headlights off as they neared the house. After he parked the car, he got out, opened Wilma's door, and extended his hand to help her out of the truck. As she hopped out of the truck, Wilma fell against Franky's chest. He wrapped his arms tightly around her and held her as she cried.

"You know what would be amazing?" He whispered.

"What?"

"What if you and I got back into the truck and just drove? Drove until we crossed the Mississippi. We could stop at a campground and rest for the night. In the morning we drive some more and stop at every little diner we see and order chocolate pie. Then we come upon some cute little town somewhere far from here and we buy a little house. It will be just you and me. None of this bullshit here."

Wilma sighed, "Oh that does sound lovely. It would be nice to get away for a bit. But I'm afraid my family would miss both of us like crazy. In a couple of weeks Dad, Angela, and I are going to visit Angela's Aunt Carol and Uncle John in some little town near Madison."

"I'm going to miss you like crazy," Franky whispered as he tightened his embrace.

"I'm going to miss you too. Thanks for being there tonight," Wilma replied as she snuggled more into Franky's chest.

After a few moments of silence, Franky asked, "Do you really think Maryanne was pulling your leg tonight?"

Wilma sighed, "I can't truly say yes, but I can't say no either. We used to be best friends, or so I thought. This summer she just got up and left our friendship."

"So you don't think she is pregnant, or you don't think it was Georgie that knocked her up?"

"If I believe all those rumors, then yes there is probably a good chance she is pregnant. I very much want to believe that it wasn't Georgie though."

Franky held Wilma's hands to his heart, "Wilma you are a good person inside and out. You know both Maryanne and Georgie better than most people do. If you want to believe what your heart believes, then that is what you do."

Wilma looked into his eyes. Damn, why does he have to be so sweet, she thought to herself.

"Good night, Franky." Wilma whispered as she kissed him on the cheek then walked inside.

13

July 28th, 1961

Dear Diary,

I am sitting in the back of Grandma and Grandpa's station wagon. Dad, Angela, and I are on the way to see her aunt and uncle in some small town. It's almost a three-hour drive from Ephraim. We will be spending the weekend with Aunt Carol and Uncle John. I hope we do something fun. I need time to clear my head. Why does love have to be so complicated?

Wilma and her family arrived in Aunt Carol and Uncle John's driveway around five that evening. Uncle John in his plaid short sleeve shirt and round belly was the first to greet them as he helped them unload their luggage from the car. He hurried them inside a sweltering kitchen where a slender woman with curly red hair was bent over pulling a steaming pot roast and potatoes out of the oven.

"Carol, look who finally made it."

Setting the roast on the hot pads she turned toward her husband. A big smile appeared on her lips and her eyes lit up. She quickly wiped her hands on her apron and pushed a chair aside so she could get to her niece.

"Angela! Hello! How is married life treating you?" Carol asked as she hugged Angela, "Turn around now, let me see you. My, don't you look beautiful and happy...And William." Carol cooed as she hugged William, "You have one happy bride. Keep up the good work, you still have many years ahead of you."

"Yes, Carol we do. Thank you for letting us stay for a couple of days," William replied as he took the luggage from John and followed him down the hallway and into the guest bedroom.

"Wilma," Carol gushed, "Wilma, you have grown into a beautiful young woman. Now tell Aunty Carol, how many boys do you have following you around."

"Aunt Carol please," Angela piped in. Wilma rolled her eyes as she stood near an open window hoping to catch the cool summer evening breeze, "We came to visit so she could get away from boys. Georgie proposed to Wilma and..." Angela leaned in and whispered, "she turned him down."

Aunt Carol gasped, "You did what?"

"Everything is just happening so fast, Aunt Carol," Wilma said, "I have a lot I need to think about. Plus, there might be another..."

"Another boy?" Aunt Carol gasped again.

"Okay, you hens, enough of this clucking. The men in this house are starving. Let's eat!" John interjected as he popped open an Old Milwaukee beer can and took a swig.

He and William sat at the small table in the kitchen. Carol separated the potatoes and carrots from the roast and whipped up some gravy from the drippings.

"Eat up now. Sitting in that station wagon for that long of a drive has made you hungry I bet. After dinner, we will relax. Got some big plans for tomorrow."

By eight o'clock the next morning it was already muggy outside. John kept wiping sweat from his brow as he showed William what was under the hood of his Peterbilt semi-truck. John had been driving semi since he and Carol had been married. He joked all the time that it was the only way their marriage was surviving.

"Have to go across the state line into Illinois and deliver a load of canned vegetables today. Care to join me, William?"

"Not today, John. This afternoon, Wilma and Angela want to check out that eccentric house that opened last year."

"Oh yes. The one that is built on that huge rock. I Haven't been there yet myself, but I hear it is a sight to see. Say, do you and Angela need any margarine? I am bringing back a case of that white Olea margarine for Carol's mom."

"Olea margarine? That bootleg margarine?"

"Will you sons of bitches keep it down out here. Now, John, I told you to leave that margarine alone. It's illegal in our state," Carol scolded them as she and the girls came outside.

"Your mom loves Olea margarine, and I want to keep her happy and off my back."

"If you get caught transporting it across state lines you could get fired. Then how will we pay our mortgage?"

"Relax will you, Carol?" John huffed as he swatted a mosquito off his arm, "One thing about living near the creek on a muggy day are these damn gnats. They are relentless this morning."

"Don't you two go touching the beer in the refrigerator now. John, you have to take a load down today."

"Yes, dear."

"Goodbye, darling," William said as he kissed Angela on the cheek, "You ladies have fun at the garage sales. Don't spend too much, okay?"

"Spend too much? Ha! William, you truly don't know women do you?" Carol snarked.

"You are correct, Aunt Carol. Try having him as your father," Wilma whined as she and the ladies headed toward the first garage sale down the street.

The afternoon mimicked the morning, hazy and muggy. Storms were popping up here and there but they didn't bring any relief to the humidity. All the windows in the station wagon were rolled down as William, Angela, Wilma, and Aunt Carol made their way to The House on the Rock. As they drove slowly through a neighborhood, William and Angela commented on the beauty of a big Victorian house. There was a front porch with a swing and a small flowerbed of daisies. A man was on a ladder touching up some blue paint around the window frame of the second story of the house. Wilma saw a boy and a girl about her age doing yard work. A woman, pulling weeds from a flowerbed, wiped the sweat from her brow as she glanced at the passing traffic. For a moment something sparked in William's mind. There was something familiar about the woman's face. His mind was racing trying to recollect something from his memory.

"William look out!" Angela suddenly screamed. William slammed on the breaks. The station wagon came to a screeching halt as it rear-ended a car stopped at a stop sign, everyone lurching forward a little from the impact.

Jolted back to reality, William checked on his family, "Everyone alright?"

"Yeah, we are fine. Damit William, didn't you see the car stop?" Carol questioned.

William looked out his window,

"I...I...thought..."

Just then the man who was painting and the driver from the other car came to the station wagon. The driver from the other car checked his back bumper, a little surprised to find just a tiny scratch. William apologized as he stepped out of his car.

"I am so sorry. Are you okay?" He asked as he placed his hand on the other driver's shoulder and glanced at the two bumpers.

The other man with blue paint on his hands asked both men if they were okay then started making small chit chat about the bumpers.

Wilma and Angela stepped out of the sweltering station wagon, "Father?" Wilma questioned.

"Everything is okay ladies, get back in the car."

"But it's so hot, there's no breeze," Wilma whined.

"Your wife and children?" William began to ask the man with blue paint on his hands.

"Yes, yes. They are fine. You gave them such a scare that they hurried inside."

"Give them my apologies. And my apologies to you," as he shook both men's hands.

"Is everything okay?" Angela asked when William got back in the car.

"Yes, just a tiny scratch on his bumper was all."

"Why didn't you stop?"

"I thought I recognized someone in the yard."

"Who would you know that lives in our small little town? Can we get going now? It's so hot in this car." Carol begged.

14

Wilma didn't find The House on the Rock very interesting and was glad to get back to Aunt Carol's house. She stood on the bank of the creek and threw pebbles into the water. Now and then a small fish would jump out of the water, catching the little gnats that floated in the air. Though the mosquitoes were horrendous, it was nice to be alone for once.

Uncle John arrived home from his deliveries around seven o'clock that night. Angela and Carol didn't feel like cooking dinner. No one complained though as there were plenty of leftovers from the pot roast and Carol whipped up her award-winning potato salad earlier that day. After the leftovers were devoured, Carol pulled out a chocolate cake she had made as a surprise the night before.

"Say, William, how about you and me go for a nice cold beer at the bar downtown after we polish off this cake?"

"Sounds great John. Honey you don't mind do you?"

"Not at all. Just be mindful of the time will you? We have to drive back home tomorrow."

Dim lighting reflected the haze of cigarette smoke that lingered in the still night air as John and William strolled into the bar. The sound of a pool ball striking another broke the outlining chatter.

"Hey, Johnny boy, how ya been?" the bartender asked as she placed his usual drink on the bar.

"Get my nephew the same will you, darling?" he asked as the bottle touched his lips. "So how is married life treating you son?"

"Pretty well, although Angela is talking about having more children," William replied.

"That is what happens when you marry someone much younger than you." John's round belly bounced as he chuckled.

"Angela is only six years younger. That isn't bad is it?"

"Depends. Do you have the energy for more children? How old is Wilma now?

"Seventeen. She will be graduating from high school this year."

"Hey you old son of a bitch," a local man interrupted, "Where you been hiding?" He asked John as they greeted each other.

As the evening passed, conversations continued, pool games were won, and the beer was going down way too easy. William swayed to the bar to grab another round for the fellas at the pool table.

"Another round ma'am," he slurred to a new bartender.

When she returned to the bar and took the money from William's hand, they made eye contact. Everything from that afternoon came rushing back to him. She was the one in the yard, on her knees taking care of the flowerbeds. She was the one he recognized but couldn't pinpoint how.

"Daisy?" he asked almost in a whisper.

"Daisy? Why...no one has called me that for years. Not since..." She placed both of her hands on the sticky bar and stared hard at William's face. She recognized those big lips. She saw that twinkle in those drunk green eyes. Memories from her youth made her smile, but only for a few seconds.

"William?" she whispered in shock

"Yes, Gwendolyn my beautiful daisy. It's me," he replied as tears welled up in his green eyes.

"William?" she questioned again as she backed away from the bar.

"Yes, Gwendolyn it's me. William Barret. Don't you remember?"

"Yes...Yes, I remember. But you died. You're dead. I watched as your ship exploded from the kamikaze plan. It was all over the television," Gwendolyn said with a still confused gaze in her eyes.

"Injured, yes, very badly. But dead no. I came back for you. Your house was empty."

"Daddy made us move...after..." she placed her hands on her belly as tears welled up in her eyes, "after the baby."

"Yes, our baby!" William shouted for joy as he stood up knocking over the barstool. He was attempting to jump over the bar and hug her when Gwendolyn's husband pushed him down.

"You son of a bitch. Leave my wife alone!"

Two men with tattoos covering their arms and cigarettes in their mouths grabbed William by the arms and dragged him to the door.

"This isn't that type of bar you asshole. We don't want your kind in here," They barked as they pushed him out the door.

"Leave him alone," Gwendolyn screamed as tears protruded down her face. Her husband, the owner of the bar, wrapped his arms around her waist and carried her into the office behind the bar.

As William fell to the ground, one of the men picked him up and punched him, making him fall to the ground for a second time. He felt the air leave his lungs as the other tattooed man kicked him in the gut. William laid on the cool sidewalk crying. Not because of the pain the guys inflicted upon him, but because of the pain he felt in his broken heart.

"Where have you been?" Angela questioned in a loud whisper as Uncle John helped William stumble through the front door, "Oh my gosh, what happened to you?" she cried as she held his blood and dirt-smudged face in her hands.

"I saw her," he answered quietly so as not to wake Wilma and Carol who were fast asleep down the hall.

"Saw who?"

"Her. I saw Gwendolyn, Wilma's birth mother."

"Don't be a fool. She's somewhere in California," Angela paused and noticed her husband couldn't even stand without swaying back and forth, "How many drinks did you have tonight? You're drunk. I asked you not to overdo it. We have to leave in the morning."

"Calm down. I will be fine in the morning," he slurred.

"Just get in the shower. I don't want to smell your drunk ass."

"I'm sorry Angela, I truly am. But I saw her. I saw her twice today. I need to speak to her. I need to tell Gwendolyn about Wilma."

"No, you don't," Angela protested angrily, "Wilma is a happy girl. She needs to focus on school this coming year. If you tell her you may mess up everything for her." she whispered in a loud octave so as not to wake

Wilma. "And as for Gwendolyn, she probably went on with her life too, just like you did. Do you want to mess up her marriage? Do you want to mess up our marriage?"

William put his hands on Angela's shoulders to balance himself. Forcing his beer breath upon her, he said, "You don't understand. She was my first love. She is Wilma's mother. Unfortunate circumstances tore us apart. I need to speak with her. I need to tell her about Wilma."

"Jesus Christ! We have only been married for eight months and you already have feelings for another woman," Angela cried angrily.

"Would you open your damn ears woman!" William shouted, "This has nothing to do with our marriage. I need to tell her about Wilma."

"What you need to do is get your sorry drunk ass in the shower. Then we are leaving. I am too pissed off to sleep now."

"Tell who about me?" Wilma said in a groggy voice as she came into the kitchen.

"Mind your business, Wilma." Angela yelled angrily, "Get your bags together. We are leaving tonight!"

15

Sunday August 20, 1961

Dear Diary,

Tomorrow I start my senior year of high school. I thought I'd be happy and excited, but I'm the total opposite. Dad and Angela have been at each other's throats for the last three weeks. I don't even know what they are fighting about. All I know is that it has something to do with me. Every time I hear them argue, they do it in hushed voices. Every time I come into the room they are in, one of them leaves, the other doesn't speak to me. Grandma says when the time is right I will find out. Until then I need to enjoy life and stop worrying about adult issues.

I can't stop worrying about adult issues though. Georgie keeps asking if I will marry him. He doesn't even want to talk about what happened at the Fourth of July beach party. I know the rumors about Maryanne being pregnant are true. Poor thing, her parents dropped her off at some religious convent place. She has to stay there until her baby is born. Georgie swears up and down he never slept with her. The night of the beach party, Franky brought me home. He said I should follow what my heart believes. My head tells my heart to believe Georgie. But my heart feels confused.

I have been staying away from the house as much as possible so I don't get in father and Angela's way and make them even angrier at each other. Even though my heart is confused, Georgie and I have been spending time together. He took me to see his apartment he will be living in at the end of the semester. It's nice for what it is but it's not as special as he makes it sound.

I've also been spending time with Franky. We take the horses out a lot. He is getting pretty good at riding. He doesn't seem nervous when he rides now, I helped him out in the barn and he took me roller skating down at the boardwalk. It was so much fun. Now that summer is coming to an end, tomorrow he and the rest of the ranch hands will leave. I am going to miss him so much. His laughter, his smile, his sweet kisses, the way he looks into my eyes, his muscles, and his fun personality is what has made this summer amazing and he has *definitely kept me from going insane these last several weeks.*

Well Diary, as this is the last page in you, I guess it's fitting to say this is how I end my summer with you. Wish me luck in my senior year Diary.

Wilma and Georgie sat cuddling in a pile of hay near the horse stalls. When they first started dating, this was a place for them to hide and be alone. One their third date, Georgie kissed her on her lips and told her she was his girl forever. Then he took his pocket knife and carved their initials in a heart on one of the wooden beams.

The moon cast a small light through the cracks in the barn walls and illuminated the heart. Wilma sighed as Georgie kissed her hand and intertwined his fingers with hers.

"Such a romantic atmosphere, isn't it?" he asked in a low sweet voice. Wilma traced his knuckles with her free hand and nodded, "Man, I wish school wasn't starting tomorrow. But just think, once this year is done, we can start our lives together as Mr. and Mrs. Brown."

Wilma untangled her hand from Georgie's. As she turned to face him, the sound of the hay rustling under her knees startled one of the horses.

"Georgie, do you ever feel like there is so much more out in this big world just waiting for you?"

"Gee, Wilma like what?"

"I don't know. Maybe something unexpected. Something you didn't think you would ever do, but the more you think about it, the more your stomach churns if you just let it pass you by."

"Are you saying you want to get married now?" he asked excitedly.

Wilma let out a small chuckled, "No...I mean..."

Georgie interrupted her, "You're worried about the war, aren't you? You think we are going to be separated and never see each other again, like your father and birth mother? The Vietnam war will be over before I turn eighteen. I'm not going anywhere."

Wilma gave Georgie a peck on the lips, "You're sweet Georgie, but that isn't what I'm saying."

"Oh no! You're pregnant. You can't be. We only had sex three times. Your father is going to kill me."

"Calm down, Georgie before you scare the horses." Wilma said, grabbing his hands, "I'm not pregnant."

"Oh, thank God!" Georgie exhaled as he put his hand on his chest and waited for his heartbeat to slow down, "Of course I'd help with the baby, our baby. I'd be a good father. We'd be good parents."

"Georgie, get a hold of yourself. I'm not talking about babies."

"Then what are you talking about, Wilma?"

One of the horses scuffed its hoof against the barn floor as a barn owl hooted up in the rafters.

"Georgie, now listen to me," Wilma said quietly, "You know how people do things because it's tradition or because people just expect it to be done a certain way? Well..."

"Oh no, Wilma, I know what you are about to do," Georgie said excitedly as he got up on his feet. He pulled Wilma up and kissed her passionately on the mouth. "I can't let you. I believe in tradition. The man is supposed to propose. I bought a ring for you. My mom helped me pick it out. The ring is sitting on my dresser. We need to do this the right way." He said as his speech and body language became more enthusiastic with each breath.

"We need to do this the right way. I know...I will come for breakfast tomorrow. I will ask your father and Angela to join us. As we are finishing up our pancakes and bacon, I will ask your father for permission to take your hand in marriage. I know he and Angela will be thrilled. Then I will take the ring box out of my pocket and get down on one knee and ask you properly."

Wilma stood speechless, her eyes huge as Georgie revealed his plan.

"Oh babe, you have made me so excited. I'm not going to be able to sleep tonight." Georgie said as he swept Wilma up in his arms and then dipped her, planting a passionate kiss on her lips, "Tomorrow morning you will be my fiance. See you at breakfast babe."

Then Georgie left Wilma standing alone in the barn. She watched as he hooted and hollered in a joyful song, disturbing all of the horses and chickens as he ran to his car. The moonlight pierced through the dust cloud of gravel as Georgie sped down the driveway, excitedly honking the horn.

Wilma stood alone in the barn, shocked by what had just happened. It took a few minutes for her to get her thoughts in order. Then she straightened her skirt and pulled bits of stray hay out of her hair as she put it up in a hair clip. She grabbed the large purse she buried in the hay and walked out of the barn.

Wilma took one last look at the farmhouse she had grown up in. Memories floated through her head as she thought about the way the Christmas tree lit up the front picture window in the winter. Many summers were spent on the back porch listening to stories her father read to her as they sipped lemonade. She thought about all the times she would sit on her grandfather's lap as he drove the tractor through the field. The tree swing gently moved in the light breeze as Wilma thought about her friendship with Maryanne. So much has changed over the summer.

Wilma was a little shocked she didn't see any lights on in the house after all the noise Georgie had made when he left. She was grateful her family was such sound sleepers. She blew a kiss towards the house and her sleeping family, "I love you all. Please don't be mad," she whispered. She took a deep breath, wiped the tears from her eyes, and walked toward the woods just beyond the barn.

"Wow, he sure seemed happy for just getting dumped," Franky said as he watched Wilma walk towards him.

Wilma sighed, "Well, he didn't exactly let me get that far."

"My truck is just parked up on the other side of those trees. Are you ready?" Franky asked as he wrapped his arms around Wilma's waist and gently touched her neck with his lips.

"You bet I am. Just let me check to make sure I haven't forgotten anything." Wilma hooked her big purse on a skinny tree branch and carefully took everything out of her bag to make sure she hadn't left anything behind. Holding the contents of the bag in her arms, she giggled as Franky whispered sweet nothings in her ear.

"Hold on Franky, I'm almost done." she laughed as she elbowed him in the stomach.

As she was placing her belongings back in her purse, Franky spun her around making her drop a book. "My diary." Wilma screeched, "Quick Franky, give me a lighter, I think it fell into the hole in the tree trunk."

Frankie lit his lighter and held it near the hole so Wilma could try to see in. "I'm sorry Babe I didn't mean to."

Wilma tried looking in the hole, sighing, she replied, "It's just…"

"I can buy you another one when we get to wherever it is we end up."

Wilma sighed, looking back at the house and then at Franky, "It's fine. Don't worry about it." She said disappointedly. " We need to leave before it gets too late."

16

The next morning Georgie arrived just in time for breakfast, but he didn't smell bacon wafting from the house as he made his way onto the porch. That's odd, he thought to himself as he knocked on the screen door. I do hope I'm not late for breakfast. I'm starving.

A distraught man came to the door, startling Georgie. Georgie cleared his throat. All of a sudden, he felt parched.

"Good morning, Mr. Barret. Not only did I come to take your lovely daughter Wilma to school today, being the first day of our senior year, but I wanted to ask you...," Georgie cleared his throat again, "I wanted to ask you, sir, for your daughter's hand in marriage."

Georgie pulled a small, gray ring box from his pocket and opened it, hoping for the approval of Mr. Barret.

"I have been saving all summer from my job at the ice cream place. See, sir, I want to propose to Wilma this morning. We plan to get married when I graduate early at the end of the first semester. Then I will go to business school. Then, next May, after Wilma graduates, we will move in together and start our life."

Georgie paused, shoving the ring box closer to Mr. Barret. Clearing his throat again, he continued, "Sir, I know…"

"It's too late son," Mr. Barret said slowly, "She's gone."

"You mean she left for school already? I told her I'd be here in the morning for…"

"No. She's gone. Here, she left this." William handed Georgie a piece of paper, "Angela found it on her pillow this morning." Mr. Barret shut the screen door leaving Georgie alone on the porch. Georgie sat on the porch and began to read.

"Dearest Father, Angela, and Grandma and Grandpa,

I love you all so very much. Please know I thought long and hard about this. I may be only seventeen, but I have grown a lot over the summer. I thought I loved Georgie and yes I thought we were going to get married after I graduated. But then I met Franky. He helped me through the tough times Georgie and I had this summer. Not once did I think I'd fall for Franky but I did and I can't apologize for that.

I grew up listening to the love story of you and my birth mother, Gwendolyn. When you were busy in the barn, I would sit in your room and go through the trunk at the end of your bed. I have seen the pictures of you and Gwendolyn. I can see the love you had for her in your eyes. I can feel the love in the letters you wrote back and forth.

I feel those same strong feelings for Franky. I know everyone thought Georgie and I would be together forever. But somewhere, somehow, what Georgie and I had faded. Franky makes me laugh and I can talk to him about anything and not feel dumb and we can be silly together. The way I feel when he wraps his arms around me, lets me know he will protect me forever, no matter what the situation is. Every time I see him smiling at me, I smile and my stomach fills with butterflies.

Father, Franky is so smart. He has been working for three summers on this farm. He has saved just about every penny he has earned. Someday he wants to go to school for engineering. He will have a good job that will provide for him and me and our family when we start one.

Please know Father that it wasn't all Franky's idea for me to leave. It was mostly mine. I know every time you look at me, you see Gwendolyn. I look just like the woman in those pictures. I know there is sadness and regret in your heart. You are a great father and I love you so much. But I don't want to feel the regret you feel.

Right now I need to spread my wings and be free. I need to be with Franky and learn all the lessons life has to throw at us. Please don't try to find me. I promise I will come home when the time is right. Please tell Georgie that I am truly sorry.

I love you so much Father,

Wilma Gwendolyn Daisy Barret.

17

PRESENT DAY.

Fireworks lit up the night sky over the old farmhouse, giving life to all the destruction left from the tornado that still needed to be cleaned up.

"Mom, if I ever run away with my true love, would you still love me?" Heidi asked.

"I don't have to worry about that because none of you are dating until you are at least thirty."

"Aww, Mom, come on be real. It's not the olden days anymore." Hayleigh joked.

"You girls don't need to worry anyway, no one will ever date you." Nicholas laughed.

"Oh, shut up. You're just mad because Molly dumped you for Tyler on the last day of school," Hayleigh scoffed.

"Kids, that's enough. It's getting late." Grandma yawned.

Nathan stood up and stretched, "Grandma, did you and Grandpa buy this farm from the Barret family?"

Grandma thought for a moment, "No. I believe it was the Johnsons."

"Well, maybe the Barret family still lives in the area. We should look them up." Heidi said.

"Oh, sweetie, I don't think so. If they were here, I think your Grandpa and I would have run into them by now. This is a small town you know," Grandma stood up and started picking up the lemonade glasses. "It's getting late and we still have a lot of cleaning up left to do tomorrow from today's storms."

"Look, guys, look!" Hayleigh exclaimed, "I typed in Barret on Facebook and look what came up, William Barret Junior, Thomas Barret, and Lawrence Barret."

"No Wilma Barret?" Heidi asked.

"Not that I see." Hayleigh sighed.

"Well, maybe she married that Franky guy. Maybe she has a different last name. Look at their friends' list and see if you can find a Wilma.

After a minute or two had passed, Hayleigh let out a loud squeal, "Oh my Gosh! Oh my Gosh! I found her."

"No way. Let me see this." Nicholas said as he pulled the cell phone out of his cousin's hand. "Grandma, we need to contact her. Wouldn't you want your diary back if someone found it."

"You are not contacting strangers this late at night young man." Grandma scolded. "Now all of you get off of your cell phones and get to bed. We have a very busy day tomorrow.

"Your Grandma is right," Grandpa said, as he and other men climbed up the porch steps.

"Those were some fine pyrotechnics this year guys," Delilah said as she kissed her husband.

"Are there any left for tomorrow night Dad?" Heidi asked.

"Let's see how much we get accomplished tomorrow."

Alex took the hands of his pregnant wife and helped her up off of the porch swing, "Are you sure you wouldn't rather stay in the motel in town instead of sleeping in the tents?"

"Alex, darling, I'm fine. I gave birth to those two goofballs over there. This little girl inside me is a piece of cake compared to them," Tammy replied, rubbing her hand over her stomach.

As everyone made their way to the tents, Hayleigh couldn't help but wonder if Wilma and her family had ever put up tents and camped on this same patch of land. She couldn't resist any longer. Knowing it was not okay to disobey her Grandma, she turned her cell phone back on, clicked the Facebook app open, and began to scroll. Finally, she began to type.

DEAR MRS. WILMA,

I AM NOT SURE IF I HAVE THE CORRECT PERSON, BUT I TRULY HOPE YOU ARE WILMA BARRET. IF YOU ARE, I HAVE YOUR DIARY. SEE, MY GRANDPARENTS LIVE IN AN OLD FARMHOUSE NEAR EPHRAIM. TODAY, THE FOURTH OF JULY, WE HAD A TORNADO RIP THROUGH TOWN. ANYWAY, WHEN WE WERE CLEANING UP MY GRANDPARENTS' LAND, I CAME ACROSS SOMETHING IN AN OLD TREE STUMP. WELL, I PULLED IT OUT AND IT WAS A BOOK. WELL, A DIARY. MY AUNT TAMMY SAID IT WAS A JOURNAL. MY COUSIN NICHOLAS THOUGHT MAYBE IT WAS OVER A HUNDRED YEARS OLD. ANYWAY, MY AUNT TAMMY READ IT TO US. SORRY FOR INVADING YOUR PRIVACY. ANYWAY, IF THIS IS THE SAME WILMA BARRET THAT WAS SEVENTEEN YEARS OLD DURING THE SUMMER OF 1961, PLEASE RESPOND.

SINCERELY, HAYLEIGH ROMERO

Hayleigh exhaled nervously. She couldn't believe she had just sent a message to a complete stranger. If this person saw the message, Hayleigh was sure they would think she was a complete lunatic. Then suddenly, three little dots on her phone screen started jumping up and down indicating the person on the other end of the message was writing back. Hayleigh could feel her heart racing as she sat waiting impatiently for the reply.

The End
The Final Chapter

The warm morning sun beat down on Wilma as she stepped up onto the porch for the first time in six years. She took a deep breath as she knocked on a white paint chipped screen door. She could hear her heart beating as she waited patiently for someone to open the door.

"Momma, you're squeezing my hand too hard," a little voice said.

"Oh darling, I'm sorry. I don't mean to," Wilma replied.

The door on the other side of the screen door opened. A little boy with messy hair and chocolate all over his face smiled.

"Hi, I'm William Junior. Who are you?"

Wilma stared at the little boy. She was suddenly speechless.

"William, get away from that door," A voice demanded as a pregnant woman with a long braid down her back came to the door.

"Can I help you?" She asked as she stared at Wilma.

"An...Angela?" Wilma stuttered nervously, "It's me, Wilma."

The woman stared at her for a second and then replied in a high pitched voice, "Wilma? Wilma! For land sakes child, come in, come in." She hugged Wilma the best she could with her protruding belly.

"How are you? Oh, your father will have a heart attack when he sees you."

"I am well," Wilma replied, still in a bit of a shock.

"Charlie, run to the barn and tell William he has company," Angela yelled to one of the ranch hands in the front yard. "Grandma, quick come see who decided to stop in for a visit." She yelled into the house as she scooted Wilma inside.

Angela knelt down and admired the little girl who was trying to hide behind Wilma. And who might you be?"

The little girl smiled as she saw William Junior sitting on the floor now, preoccupied with a piece of chocolate cake. She grabbed the sides of her dress, "I'm McKenzie. I'm five." she said as she curtsied.

"Oh Wilma, she is adorable. She looks just like you," Angela gushed.

Just then Grandma and William appeared in the dining room.

"What's all the fuss, Angela?" he asked as he wiped the sweat from his forehead with his handkerchief.

Angela stepped aside so Wilma could get a look at her father.

"Hi Father, it's me, Wilma," she said with a smile as tears began to roll down her cheeks.

William looked bewildered as he stared at Wilma.

"And I'm McKenzie. I'm five." McKenzie pipped in breaking the awkward silence.

"Wilma? Wilma! Oh, Wilma." William cried as he made his way to his daughter and gave her a big hug, "We thought we'd never see you again."

"I'm sorry, Father. I'm so sorry. But I had to leave. I had to make a life of my own," she cried as she hugged her father.

"I know, child, I know," William replied as he stroked the back of his daughter's head. Then he gently pushed her away and knelt down so he was face to face with McKenzie. He shook her hand as he said, "Hi McKenzie. I'm William," He looked up at Wilma as she smiled and nodded her head, "I'm your grandpa."

McKenzie looked at William and said, "Can I have some cake like that boy?"

Everybody laughed. Angela hurried into the kitchen and returned to the dining room with a small piece of chocolate cake for McKenzie.

"And Franky?" William asked as he motioned for everyone to sit at the dining room table.

"Franky is wonderful." Wilma smiled, "He is actually out in the car. He wasn't sure how you would react when we showed up on your front porch."

Everyone laughed again. Then William took his daughter's hand and led her to the front door. Together they waved until Franky made his way out of the car. He was greeted on the porch with a handshake from William and a hug from Grandma.

The family spent the rest of the day getting caught up. Franky and Wilma shared the good news that Franky had accepted a job in the city and that they had just bought a house outside of the city. William and Angela talked about what it was like having children after all these years. They shared how Grandpa was ready to sell the farm and enjoy the time he and Grandma had left.

That evening, Wilma helped her grandmother and Angela fix sloppy joes and potato salad for supper. Franky and William spent time in the barn, getting to know each other as father and son-in-law. McKenzie and William Jr. chased the chickens in the yard and played tag until everyone was called in for dinner.

After dinner, Grandma and Angela offered to take the kids up to the bathroom and bathe them, while Franky and Grandpa cleaned up the kitchen. William and Wilma shared a pitcher of lemonade out on the porch swing as they watched the lightning bugs come out.

"I have something to tell you, Wilma," William said after a while.

"What's that, Father?"

"I um...I...well, I saw Gwendolyn a few years ago."

"Oh my God. What did you say? What did she say? Did you tell her about me?"

"Oh, Wilma," William replied as he set his lemonade down on the side table and turned towards his daughter.

"Wilma I truly wanted to, but I think she and I would be heartbroken, knowing we couldn't be together anymore. She is married and has a family of her own. Angela and I are married and we have started having children again. I still love Gwendolyn, even after all these years, I can't bear the thought that if I talked to her, and told her about you, that it might ruin her marriage and tear her family apart." William paused for a moment, "Sometimes, if you truly love somebody, you have to let them go," he said quietly as tears rolled down his sunburned face.

"Where did you see her? Where does she live.?" Wilma clamored.

But her father shook his head, "Her whereabouts will die with me, Wilma. Like I said, if you truly love somebody, you will let them go. Someday, if it's meant to be, our families will come together. But for now, I have to accept that the memories I have of Gwendolyn will have to live in my heart for the rest of my life. I am blessed to have you and McKenzie back in my life. You look so much like Gwendolyn. And little McKenzie looks so much like you did at the age of five."

William finished his glass of lemonade and then stood up. He kissed his daughter on the head, "Please, for Gwendolyn's sake, leave her be," Then he walked inside and left Wilma alone for the night with her thoughts.

And so ends the story of William, Gwendolyn and their daughter Wilma.

ACKNOWLEDGMENTS

I would like to thank my editors Joan, Michelle, and Sandy. I know editing is tedious but you three willingly took time out of your busy lives to read the whole story or parts of the story. I thank you all so much for your honesty, your opinions, and your help with this story. I also want to thank you for being flexible to video chat or text about the story since we couldn't get together during this Covid-19 pandemic.

I also want to thank my Creative Cover Design Team Dawn, Leona, and Sierra. Thank you for your honesty and thoughts on the book cover. I know it's hard to make decisions when the picture is on a computer screen and isn't always the best clarity. After many decisions, I love the cover that was chosen.

And lastly, I want to thank my Aunt Jackie for the tidbits of family information I was able to add to the story. The information adds familiarity and makes some of the characters very relatable. It was fun writing the information into the story.

Big Thanks Yous and Hugs to all of you!

ABOUT THE AUTHOR

This is Heather's second book. When not writing, Heather enjoys the challenges of raising two teenagers with her husband of almost twenty years. Heather also enjoys acting in community theater and working in her tranquil flowerbeds and vegetable garden. She hopes to one day buy a house in the country with enough land to raise more chickens and adopt some goats. Heather hopes you will fall in love with the characters of this story just like you did with the characters in her first book, *A Love Tucked Away in the Attic*.

For updates on new books, FAQ's and fun tidbits about my other books, check out my websites.

www.heatherrobersonsbookself.wordpress.com

www.amazon.com/author/heatherroberson